Worcester American antiquarian society

The Bradford Manuscript

Worcester American antiquarian society

The Bradford Manuscript

ISBN/EAN: 9783742810304

Manufactured in Europe, USA, Canada, Australia, Japa

Cover: Foto ©Andreas Hilbeck / pixelio.de

Manufactured and distributed by brebook publishing software
(www.brebook.com)

Worcester American antiquarian society

The Bradford Manuscript

THE BRADFORD MANUSCRIPT.

ACCOUNT OF THE PART TAKEN BY THE

American Antiquarian Society

IN THE RETURN OF THE

BRADFORD MANUSCRIPT

TO AMERICA.

Worcester, Mass., U. S. A.

PRESS OF CHARLES HAMILTON.

311 MAIN STREET.

1898.

NOTE BY THE COMMITTEE OF PUBLICATION.

THE important part taken by the AMERICAN ANTI-QUARIAN SOCIETY, at the instigation of its first Vice-President, Senator HOAR, in inaugurating and securing the return of the BRADFORD MANUSCRIPT to the United States and its deposit in the custody of the Common-wealth of Massachusetts, has made it seem fitting that some account should be printed, relating the particulars of the successful undertaking and describing the exercises therewith connected.

The Committee is indebted to the Secretary of the Commonwealth for the use of the portraits herewith presented.

CONTENTS.

ACTION OF THE SOCIETY.

ACTION OF THE AMERICAN ANTIQUARIAN SOCIETY.

At a meeting of the Council, held October 9, 1896, Vice-President Hoar stated that the Manuscript of Governor Bradford's History was in possession of the Lord Bishop of London, and he was encouraged to believe that if proper application were made it might be restored to this country.

At a meeting of the Council, held October 20, 1896, on motion of Vice-President Hoar it was

Voted, that the President appoint a committee of three members of the Society who shall obtain the coöperation of the Massachusetts Historical Society, the Pilgrim Society at Plymouth, and the Governor of the Commonwealth in making application, through the American Ambassador at London, to the Lord Bishop of London, for the restoration to Massachusetts of the original Manuscript of Bradford's History of the Pilgrim Plantation, now in possession of the Lord Bishop of London.

Voted, that the President be one of the committee.

The Committee as appointed consisted of President Stephen Salisbury, Vice-Presidents George F. Hoar and Edward E. Hale, and Benjamin A. Gould, LL.D.

2

At a special meeting of the Council, held May 18, 1897, it was

Voted, that the American Antiquarian Society tender to the Governor of the Commonwealth, the Hon. Thomas F. Bayard and such other invited guests as a committee may select, a dinner in Boston on the occasion of the reception of the Bradford Manuscript by the Commonwealth.

Voted, that the President, Dr. Samuel A. Green and Arthur Lord, Esq., be a committee of arrangements with full power and with liberty to add to their number.

Nathaniel Paine and Francis C. Lowell were subsequently added to the committee.

The committee sent out the following invitation:

THE AMERICAN ANTIQUARIAN SOCIETY.

WORCESTER, *May 20th, 1897.*

The Council of the American Antiquarian Society request your presence at a collation at the Parker House, Boston, on Wednesday, Twenty-Sixth instant, at 2 o'clock P. M., to celebrate the gracious return of the Bradford Manuscript to the Commonwealth of Massachusetts by Great Britain, and to meet His Excellency Governor Roger Wolcott, Honorable Thomas F. Bayard and Honorable George F. Hoar.

Very respectfully yours,

STEPHEN SALISBURY.
SAMUEL A. GREEN.
ARTHUR LORD.
NATHANIEL PAINE.
FRANCIS C. LOWELL.

At a meeting of the Council, held October 2, 1897, it was

Voted, that the matter of publishing an account of the proceedings in connection with the reception of the Bradford Manuscript be referred to the Publishing Committee and to Vice-President Hoar, with power to act.

In accordance with the vote of the Council a dinner was given at the Parker House, Boston, on Wednesday, May 26, 1897, at which the following gentlemen were present:

INVITED GUESTS.

His Excellency Governor ROGER WOLCOTT.

Hon. THOMAS F. BAYARD.

His Honor W. MURRAY CRANE, Lieutenant-Governor.

Hon. GEORGE P. LAWRENCE, President Massachusetts Senate.

Right Reverend WILLIAM LAWRENCE, D.D., Bishop of Massachusetts.

Reverend GEORGE A. GORDON, D.D.

Sir DOMINIC COLNAGHI, British Consul at Boston.

CHARLES C. BEAMAN, President of the New England Society of New York.

Hon. JOHN WINSLOW, President of the New England Society of Brooklyn.

GAMALIEL BRADFORD, a descendant of Governor Bradford.

WILLIAM T. DAVIS, Pilgrim Society, Plymouth.

MEMBERS OF THE AMERICAN ANTIQUARIAN SOCIETY.

Hon. STEPHEN SALISBURY, President.

Hon. GEORGE F. HOAR and Rev. EDWARD E. HALE, D.D.,
Vice-Presidents.

THE BANQUET.

THE BANQUET.

At the close of the Banquet PRESIDENT SALISBURY addressed the company as follows :

Gentlemen of the Society and Honored Guests :

After the enjoyment of the exercises of this morning, and filled with the emotions excited by the gracious return of the original Bradford manuscript history of Pilgrim wanderings and establishment at Plymouth, it seems fitting that this Society should congratulate itself that it was primarily through the suggestion, exceeding tact and delicate diplomacy of its first Vice-President, Senator George F. Hoar, that negotiations were set on foot and continued, until at length this Commonwealth again possesses the earliest original documentary record of colonization upon the American continent. This priceless volume, written by the illustrious William Bradford ten years after the arrival of the *Mayflower* on our shores, after strange vicissitudes, was discovered in the library of the Bishop of London at Fulham, and by his permission and the decree of the Consistorial Court has been most freely given back to the Commonwealth of Massachusetts, and entrusted to the care of Ex-Ambassador Thomas F. Bayard, for presentation to the Executive of the Commonwealth. The honors of this day are rightly given to those who in various ways have so nobly coöperated in securing this precious talisman ; but we must not forget that without the efforts of our distinguished Senator and Vice-President, we should not have met for this delightful occasion.

In accordance with custom the first toast that I will propose is the President of the United States, and the responsive feelings of this gathering can best be shown by the company's rising in recognition of the supreme position of the first officer of this country.

The entire company rose in response and drank to the health of the President of the United States of America.

President Salisbury then said:

The Governor of the Commonwealth has addressed the two branches of the Legislature today in a manner so fitting, and indicating so clearly his appreciation of the historical value of the unique treasure that has been recovered, that aside from our testimony of respect for his high official station, we desire to manifest to him our hearty sentiments of personal good will. The Governor of the Commonwealth, His Excellency Roger Wolcott.

Governor Wolcott said:

Mr. President and Gentlemen of the American Antiquarian Society: I hardly know how I can add anything to the impressive and dignified occasion of the morning. I was honored, by my official position, in being able to have a part, however insignificant, in bringing about the decree of the Consistorial and Ecclesiastical Court of London that led to the restoration of this History to the keeping of the people of whose early struggles it tells.

For this the Commonwealth owes a debt to her senior Senator, and I feel privileged, on the part of the Commonwealth, to express her indebtedness to Mr. Bayard for so successfully having followed out the suggestion.

The element of pathos noticeable in the book is wiped out in victory. It is not a dirge swelling from this volume, but a pæan of victory.

Today the Commonwealth adds to its possessions a priceless treasure. It has been a day of profound significance as a day marking an important epoch in the history

ROGER WOLCOTT.

of Massachusetts. It will not be a dull and lifeless possession, but an inspiration to good citizenship.

In announcing the third toast President Salisbury said:

We have assurance that by the most gracious permission
of her Majesty, Queen Victoria, the treasure that we have
this day had returned to us was freely accorded; and this
act of the noble lady is in harmony with the uniform
promptings of her exalted character, and is such a renewed
manifestation of her friendly disposition toward this
country that it is with feelings of the highest respect and
gratitude that this Society now desires to propose the
health of her most gracious Majesty, the Queen. I will
call upon the British Consul, Sir Dominic Colnaghi, to
respond.

After the company had risen and drank to the health
of the Queen, Consul-General Colnaghi responded as follows:

Mr. President and Gentlemen: I came here today on
the courteous invitation of the American Antiquarian
Society to meet some distinguished Americans and, as I
thought, to listen, tranquilly, to some interesting speeches.
Most unexpectedly I have been called upon to speak
myself. I have been suddenly exalted; I trust I may not,
shortly, be abased.

The noble words spoken, this morning, of the Queen of
England, by Senator Hoar, have, doubtless, already been
flashed across the Atlantic, and by this time are being
read, with feelings of deep gratification, by every Briton.
Gentlemen, there is a tender feeling in the hearts of my
countrymen for the State of Massachusetts, and there is a
feeling of deep and hearty good will towards this great
Republic. May we not, indeed, in great part consider you
as our child and regard you as a natural offshoot of British
law, British energy and British love of freedom?

I am sure that the Queen will hear of what has been said today with the greatest interest; and I thank you, very heartily, for the manner in which you have responded to the toast of Her Majesty's health.

I have learnt that the title "Log of the Mayflower" as applied to the Bradford Manuscript is incorrect. It may, however, be considered a graceful coincidence that the present ceremony has occurred on the birthday of our English Mayflower — the Princess May — now the Duchess of York.

Will you allow me, in conclusion, to thank you most truly for all that has, this day, been said of England.

President Salisbury then said:

The details of diplomatic courtesy, so important in a negotiation like that regarding the return of the manuscript, were entrusted to the care of Ex-Ambassador, the Honorable Thomas F. Bayard, and the entire harmony that seemed to attend all interviews and formal ceremonies, is proof that skill in diplomacy is appreciated, when possessed by our accredited agents abroad. As one to whom we owe so much of today's enjoyment, I will call upon our first ambassador to England, the Honorable Thomas F. Bayard.

Mr. Bayard was received with great applause, and said:

I feel honored by the invitation to join the American Antiquarian Society at this agreeable repast. For the part I have had in the restoration of the manuscript of Governor Bradford to the people and the State that his adventure founded, I am well rewarded by my own reflections; and if there had been no formal reception I should have been gratified in every way by the fact that I had it in my power to assist in the return of this volume to my country-men who are its legitimate owners.

Mr. Bayard spoke of the change in the title of the representative of the government to the court of St. James from minister to that of ambassador, and remarked :

But it did not change the American republic or those who represented it in the eyes of those to whom I was sent.

Massachusetts has had an enviable reputation abroad. You have had the three Adamses as honorable representatives to the court of St. James. You have had a man whose name no one would mention but with respect and of whom no son of Massachusetts would speak but with affection—James Russell Lowell. Then I could mention Abbott Lawrence and J. Lothrop Motley, and the name and pen of Nathaniel Hawthorne which have shed lustre upon New England ; and my personal friend, Edward J. Phelps, has added distinction to the public service. I only mention this to say that no mere title of ambassador would have made these men more respected, for they were respected because they were honorable Americans.

As you know, my home is in another state, although I have much to attract me to New England, inasmuch as my grandchildren live here. But it so happened that I have not been to New England as often as I could have wished.

Mr. Bayard spoke of the gratification he felt as ambassador in participating personally during his term of service in England in three events that had especial interest for Massachusetts, — the unveiling of the memorial window to John Eliot, the apostle to the Indians, at Wickford ; the laying of the corner-stone of the memorial church to John Robinson at Gainsborough, and the return of the Bradford Manuscript.

When I had the book in my possession, said Mr. Bayard, or rather when the book had me in its possession, on my way across the ocean, I thought of the journey which its writer first made, of that weary, tempestuous voyage.

Then I contrasted it with the ocean trip on board the modern steamer, on the deck of which the Mayflower and her cargo could have been stowed away, and which required days instead of weeks for the voyage. It is those things, what our German friends call the object lessons, that show us what has been accomplished. Here you have the vast chasm of time between those two voyages bridged over, and the marvelous events that have now passed into history and can never be forgotten.

The incidents I have mentioned were pleasant incidents in the duties which occupied my time while in England. Of what I did there and of what I tried to do, I shall not speak. The record is made up, and I shall stand upon it.

I am very sure of one thing, and that is that when the true history of these four years is written, when the relations of our country and England are more clearly understood, it will be seen that the good feeling has been advanced, not by formal instruments and statutes so much as by the people. There may be petty animosities and racial prejudices and appeals to ancient feuds and trade jealousies, but it cannot divert the current. There is an affinity of morals, of ethics, a similarity of the standards of justice, of right and wrong, between those who speak the English language, and the man who does not perceive it, or who seeks to thwart it, is bound to be swept aside.

President Salisbury said:

The cordial approval and assistance of the Bishop of London, whose slightest objection would have created insuperable obstacles, should now be properly recognized. I will call upon Right Reverend William Lawrence to respond.

Bishop Lawrence said:

As Senator Hoar was telling us this morning the story of the return of the manuscript and the courtesy extended

THOMAS F. BAYARD.

by the past Lord Bishop of London, now His Grace the
Archbishop of Canterbury, and the present Lord Bishop
of London, I could not help thinking how the varied interests of civilization are inextricably interwoven. These
gentlemen are ecclesiastics, they are also men of letters
and historic sense: they are loyal subjects of the Queen
and lovers of mankind. When, therefore, the request for
the return of the manuscript came to them, their historic
sense appreciated the fitness of granting the request, their
ecclesiastical position gave them the opportunity, their loy-
alty to their own country helped them to realize how loyal
we are to the traditions of our own land, and their love of
mankind prompted them to this gracious act that by mutual
courtesy and sacrifice the bonds between nation and nation
may be made strong.

Our thoughts today have run far beyond the Bradford
manuscript and have touched the sweep of international
relations and especially of our relations with the mother
country. The Lord Bishop of London was, we remember,
the representative of John Harvard's college, Emmanuel,
at the two hundred and fiftieth anniversary of Harvard
College. He carried back to England with him an honorary
degree and the regard of all those who met him. He is a
member of the American Antiquarian Society and a corre-
sponding member of the Massachusetts Historical Society.
These literary associations are also international bonds.

We regret deeply the defeat of the Arbitration Treaty.
But stronger than any treaty, in fact essential to the consideration of any treaty, are the millions of threads which
intertwined make a cable between land and land that no
cheap politics or war fever can break.

Religion, letters, art, social sympathy and all other
interests of civilization go to make up this lovers' knot
between nation and nation. Every scholar, theologian and
artist, every student of social life, every society for historical, scientific or professional research is taking part by

correspondence, courtesy and sympathy in welding the nations together.

The two great English speaking nations have everything to gain by mutual confidence and good will. Such an act of courtesy on the part of the Bishop of London, representing the people of England, cannot stand as an isolated event, but touches the sentiment of the citizens of both countries.

God grant that by untold numbers of strands of good will and sacrifice these two nations may be bound together as leaders in Christian civilization and exemplars to other peoples of the wisdom as well as righteousness of nations like brethren dwelling together in unity.

President Salisbury said:

The Pilgrim Society, having its seat in Plymouth, containing in its membership many lineal descendants of the Mayflower settlement, and possessing the richest collection of relics of the Bradford period, more than any organization has reason to be grateful today at the return of a document unique in character, as the earliest original record of settlement in America, written in the legible and carefully chosen language of the first governor of the Plymouth Colony. I will call upon Mr. Arthur Lord, President of the Pilgrim Society.

Mr. Lord said:

Mr. President: In behalf of the Pilgrim Society, which was organized three-quarters of a century ago to perpetuate the memory of the virtue, the enterprise and the sufferings of those first settlers at Plymouth and which still preserves such memorials of the early days as the hand of time has spared, and in behalf also of the Town of Plymouth, if as a citizen I may speak for it, a town whose people are more interested than any other in the grateful observances of this day, I desire to express the acknowledg-

ments of the Society and of the Town to Senator Hoar and
Mr. Bayard for their generous and successful efforts in
securing the return of the Bradford Manuscript.

It is a debt which we can never repay and which we
shall never forget.

I had hoped, Mr. President, when the petition was prepared and presented asking for the restoration to Massachusetts of the History of "Plimoth Plantation," and
especially when the report of the proceedings was first
received and it was there stated that the American Ambassador had suggested as a proper place of deposit of the
manuscript, the Pilgrim Hall in Plymouth, that if the
request of the petitioners were granted it might be possible to select as its final resting-place some spot within the
limits of the Old Colony, of whose history it is the
authoritative record and on whose soil it was written by
the hand of one, who, as its governor, shaped its destiny
in the earlier years.

But today I cheerfully recognize, in view of the statement of Mr. Bayard, that after all, its return was not based
upon any legal right of ours to receive, or upon any moral
obligation or duty on their part to give, but must rest and
rest alone on those strong lines of friendship and kindly
feeling between the two great peoples, united by the common ties of language and blood, and as an expression of
international courtesy as grateful as it is fitting.

The people of Plymouth have entire confidence that the
Governor, to whom has been entrusted, under the terms
of the decree, the duty of selecting its final resting-place,
will wisely decide and that he will select that spot where
it ever will be most carefully preserved and tenderly
cherished.

Mr. Salisbury said:

The New England Society of New York delights in all
historical matters of colonial times and is especially inter-

ested in this occasion. I will ask Mr. Charles C. Beaman,
its President, to respond for the Society.

Mr. Beaman said:

Mr. President and Gentlemen: I have had great pleasure as one of your guests in attending the very interesting
services at the State House this morning and in being at
this banquet. The New England Society of New York
has had a special part in the happiness of today because
having had the privilege of joining, through its President
and through its Ex-Presidents, Mr. Evarts, Mr. Choate
and Mr. Morgan, in the memorial asking the return of the
Governor Bradford Manuscript, it now feels that it has a
certain right to join in the thanks and in the congratula-
tions and in the general rejoicings.

We New Englanders in New York will long be happy
with you and with New Englanders everywhere that this
precious manuscript is forever to be guarded here, and
that to this manuscript our children for ages may come
with reverence and here give thanks that they are de-
scended from those noble men and women who landed
from the *Mayflower* or from those other ships that soon
followed her. The Governor Bradford record will never
grow dull. We are just now all reading Nansen's book,
Farthest North, giving the story of the voyage of the
Fram, and we are thrilled as we read, but the voyage
of the *Fram* was a mere picnic as compared with the
voyage of the *Mayflower*. On the *Fram* was health, com-
fort, almost luxury, and men. On the *Mayflower* was
sickness, scarcity, and crowded men, women and children;
and then compare the Bradford record of that first winter
at Plymouth with Nansen's story of the drifting of the
Fram for six months in the ice. Not a death on the
Fram and nearly half dead of those from the *Mayflower*.

I congratulate you that this manuscript is now again our
treasure. The manner of its finding, the graciousness of

its return, have greatly added to its value, and I feel that we can truly say : 'Tis better it was lost and found than never to have been lost at all.

For myself and for the New England Society of New York I thank you for all the pleasure of this day.

Mr. Salisbury said :

The Massachusetts Historical Society, which claims the honor of being the oldest historical organization in this country, as it held its first regular meeting in 1791, and became custodian of a wealth of manuscripts and records of old colony times, is largely represented at this banquet today. I will ask Dr. Justin Winsor, Vice-President of the Massachusetts Historical Society, to respond for the Society.

Dr. Winsor responded briefly and said he had many years ago seen the manuscript in the library of the Bishop of London and with Mr. Motley made an unsuccessful attempt to obtain it.

Mr. Salisbury in introducing Senator Hoar said :

We know what we have enjoyed today and we realize the fact that but for the ability and discretion of one of our associates our presence would not have been desired, nor would there have been any occasion for our presence. Few scholars have a disposition for historical investigation so born in them as our associate to whom we have listened today with so much edification, and we are only too glad to recognize in the Honorable George F. Hoar, the senior Senator from Massachusetts, a determination to pursue the scrutiny of material untiringly, until absolute truth and accuracy are reached. I have the honor to present the first Vice-President of the American Antiquarian Society, The Honorable George F. Hoar.

Senator Hoar spoke as follows :

Mr. President: You ask me to end the proceedings of

3

this interesting day by a few words in behalf of the American Antiquarian Society.

I am sorry, as the Vice-President and once the President of that Society, to say that in one respect it has been a great failure. It has failed to answer the expectation of Isaiah Thomas, its founder and first President. As you well know, he founded the Society in 1812. That was just at the beginning of our last war with England. He provided that our collections and library should always be kept at Worcester, forty miles from the seaboard. That was, as we all know, that they might not be captured by the British, as he thought would not be unlikely to happen if they were in Boston.

But now, eighty-five years afterward, not only the whole Society, but the whole Commonwealth of Massachusetts, has been captured by two English bishops. John Milton, in describing our ancestors' departure, in a well known passage, said that they "fled from the fury of the bishops," and yet what the fury of the bishops could not do, what the whole fleet and army of England could not do, the good will of two kindly, excellent prelates has at last accomplished. They have taken all Massachusetts. The spiritual influence from which Bradford fled, wielded in large part by the successor of Archbishop Laud, rendered mild and gentle by the spirit of our day, has taken captive, not only the American Antiquarian Society, but the whole Commonwealth.

Mr. President, there is no greater mistake than the prevalent notion that there is a feeling of animosity between the people of England and the people of America. I have lately made two trips abroad. I have seen people of all classes in England. I can say what Mr. Bayard will also say, that the feeling among Englishmen for America is such that although my nationality was well known I have never heard an unkind, I had almost said I had never heard a cold word, spoken by an Englishman.

The people who represent the different classes in England, the business men, the merchants, the workingmen, the gentry, Englishmen of every character and occupation, are in the main lovers of the people of the United States. The people of the United States, notwithstanding what may be said in the press and in foolish and exaggerated political argument, are in the main lovers of their kindred beyond the sea.

Our accomplished friend, Mr. Winsor, told us just now of his conversation by telephone with the editor of a great New York daily. Mr. Winsor is a very bold man. He evidently does not expect any important office, just at present. He was bold enough to tell the editor that "he had listened to a very foolish story." Now, if any New York editor or New York correspondent of a London editor thinks there is hatred, there is prejudice, there is a feeling of jingoism, prevailing to any great extent in the United States toward England, he has listened to a very foolish story.

My friend, Bishop Lawrence, referred to one of the chief regrets of my own public life, — the failure of the arbitration treaty. I cannot, of course, speak of what happened in the executive session of the Senate. But if the newspapers are right, and whether they are right or not I must not undertake to tell you, after that treaty had been amended so as to correspond almost exactly to Lord Salisbury's original desire, a desire which he very reluctantly yielded in his discussions with Mr. Olney, the treaty came within three votes of receiving a two-thirds vote in the Senate, or would have been saved by a change of three votes. Whether this be true or not I will not say. But this is what the newspapers tell you.

If the newspapers are right the treaty was defeated chiefly by the votes of the states lately in rebellion and the sparsely settled new states which were but a short time ago a wilderness. The great majorities of the Ameri-

can population are, in my opinion, heartily in accord with
the spirit of peace and good will by which that treaty
was inspired.

Why! that English island is half ours. Its story is the
story of our ancestry. Its history, its eight hundred years
of advancement towards civil and religious liberty, is ours
also. We are inheritors of its fame. Upon its loveliness
the eyes of our ancestors gazed. We have a share in its
beautiful temples. I never look without a feeling of love
and a thrill of delight upon those magnificent cathedrals,
and without being tempted to exclaim,

> "Oh, pull not down those palace towers, which are
>   So lightly, beautifully built."

The beautiful parish churches with the holy ground
about them hold the dust of our ancestors as well as theirs.
How they seem to have grown into the landscape as if the
very stones loved to be there!

As our friend has said, the utterances of today will be
read across the sea. If any Englishman is to read what is
said today, I am glad to be able to utter as the last word
in this day of the jubilee of that gracious Queen — the
Queen, God bless her; England, God preserve her.

[*From Proceedings of the Society, October, 1897.*]

Rev. Edward E. Hale said:

A year ago, when we were here, our senior Vice-President reported to us the condition and prospect of the
Bradford Manuscript. In the year which has passed we
have had the great happiness of receiving the manuscript
in a stately ceremonial which was really worthy of the
occasion, and I have prepared this resolution :

Resolved, That the thanks of this Society be presented
to our Senior Vice-President, Senator Hoar, for the part
which he has taken in returning the Bradford Manuscript
to this country ; we recognize the value of his services from

the beginning to the end, and assure him that his name will always be remembered by all patriots who use this first record of our public history.

This resolution was unanimously adopted.

—

The following letter from the Archbishop of Canterbury finds a fitting place here :

LAMBETH PALACE, S. E., *11 June, 1897.*

MY DEAR SIR :

I am indeed most gratified for the kindness you have shown in sending the account of the proceedings at the reception of the Bradford Manuscript by the Governor of Massachusetts. And the words used at that reception by yourself and by the other speakers will long burn in many English hearts as expressing the warm feelings which so many Americans cherish toward the Mother Country. Be assured that the strong respect and affection which is felt in England towards the Great Republic of the West, our pride in your greatness, and desire for your good will, although they may wax and wane as human things inevitably do, yet will never perish. I pray God to bless the deep felt sympathy that links our hearts to yours and binds us closer together than any other two nations ever were or ever will be bound.

Believe me

Yours very sincerely,

F. CANTUAR.

The Honorable G. F. HOAR.

RETURN OF THE MANUSCRIPT.

.

THE RETURN OF THE MANUSCRIPT OF BRADFORD'S HISTORY.

BY GEORGE F. HOAR.

THE American Antiquarian Society had so large a share in procuring the restoration of the Bradford Manuscript, that its Proceedings seem to be a proper place to record the facts connected with this most interesting transaction.

The story of the discovery of this long-lost document, in the library of the Bishop of London at Fulham, was narrated by our associate, Mr. Charles Deane, in the introduction to the edition of Bradford's History, published by the Massachusetts Historical Society in 1856 (Mass. Hist. Soc. Collections, 4th Series, Vol. 3); and by our associate, Mr. Justin Winsor, in a paper published by the same society in 1883. (Mass. Hist. Soc. Proceedings, Vol. 19.) Mr. Winsor has also given an account of some former attempts to procure the restoration of the manuscript to this country, in the Proceedings of the Massachusetts Historical Society, April, 1897.

These narratives are easily accessible and seem sure of lasting preservation. It is not necessary to repeat them here.

The writer was called upon to deliver an oration at Plymouth, December 21, 1895, on the Two Hundred and Seventy-fifth Anniversary of the Landing. In the discharge of that duty he, of course, read Governor Bradford's narrative again, with a new and enthusiastic admiration for his character, and the simple dignity and beauty with which he tells the noble story.

From this came the new and successful attempt, an account of which was given to the Legislature when the manuscript was received by the Governor, in the presence of the two Houses, as set forth herein.

The writer's conversation with Bishop Temple was reported to the Council of the American Antiquarian Society at a meeting in the autumn of 1896. The Council authorized the President to appoint a committee to join in the application. Like committees were appointed by the Massachusetts Historical Society, the Pilgrim Society of Plymouth and the New England Society of New York. The following letter, signed by the several committees, was addressed to the Bishop of London and transmitted to him through Ambassador Bayard :

> WORCESTER, Massachusetts, U. S. A.,
> *December 21, 1896.*

TO THE RIGHT REV. THE BISHOP OF LONDON.

MY LORD : We have been directed by the American Antiquarian Society, the Massachusetts Historical Society, the Pilgrim Society of Plymouth, and the New England Society of New York, with the coöperation of the Governor of the Commonwealth of Massachusetts, to call your Lordship's attention to the manuscript history of William Bradford now in the Library at Fulham, and to ask that your Lordship direct that it be given to the American Ambassador to be by him restored to Massachusetts.

The author of this manuscript was Governor William Bradford, the second Governor of Plymouth Colony, and one of the leaders of the band of pilgrims who left England in 1608, and after dwelling for thirteen years in Holland, crossed the Atlantic in the *Mayflower*, and made the first English settlement in what is now the United States of America, with the exception of the settlement at Jamestown, Virginia, which was subsequently abandoned. This manuscript is justly regarded by Americans as a precious relic. It contains the history of the formation of Plymouth Colony, of the voyage of the Pilgrims in the *Mayflower*, of the landing at Plymouth, and of the first twenty-eight years of the Colony. If there should be found a manuscript history in the handwriting of King Alfred of his own reign and of the conflict with the Danes in which he was the leader, it could hardly be more precious to Englishmen than this manuscript is to Americans.

The history of the document, so far as it is known, is contained in an ancient inscription which you will find on the fly-leaf, as follows :

"This book was writ by Governor William Bradford and given to his son, Major William Bradford and by him to his son, Major John Bradford, writ by me Samuel Bradford, March 20th., 1705."

On the next leaf is the following :

"TUESDAY, *June 4th.*, 1728.

"Calling at Major John Bradford's at Kingston near Plimouth, son of Major Wm. Bradford formerly Dep. Gov'r. of Plimouth Colony, who was eldest son of Wm. Bradford, their 2d. Gov'r. & author of this History ; — ye sd Major John Bradford gave me Several Manuscript Octavoes wh he assured me were written with his said grandfather Gov'r Bradford's own Hand. He also gave me a little pencil book wrote with a blew lead pencil by his sd Father ye Dep. Gov'r and He also told me yt He had lent and only lent his sd grandfather Gov'r Bradford's History of Plimouth Colony wrote by his own Hand, also, to Judge Sewall ; and desired me to get it of Him or find it out, & take out of it what I think proper for my New England Chronology : wh I accordingly obtained and This is ye sd History : wh I find wrote in ye same Hand writing as ye Octavo Manuscript above sd.

"THOMAS PRINCE.

"N. B. I also mentioned to him my desire of lodging this History in ye New England Library of Prints and Manuscripts wh I had been then collecting for 23 years, to wh he signified his willingness only yt He might have ye perusal of it while He lived.

"T. PRINCE."

This inscription follows:

THIS BOOK BELONGS TO
THE NEW ENGLAND LIBRARY
BEGUN TO BE COLLECTED BY THOMAS PRINCE
UPON HIS ENTERING HARVARD COLLEGE, JULY 6
1703; AND WAS GIVEN BY

IT NOW BELONGS TO THE BISHOP OF
LONDON'S LIBRARY AT FULHAM.

These inscriptions seem to make it clear that the manuscript belongs to the Prince Library. That Library was given by the Rev. Thomas Prince, who collected it, to the Old South Church in Boston. Prince was an eminent scholar and antiquary. So the case would seem to be that of a valuable manuscript belonging to one library having by some unexplained accident got into another library.

The Prince Library became the property of the Old South Church in Boston, and has been recently deposited by that church in the public library of the City of Boston, one of the largest and best libraries in the United States, where it is likely to remain.

It is not certainly known how the manuscript came to the Library at Fulham. Some persons conjecture that Thomas Hutchinson, Governor of Massachusetts just before the breaking out of the Revolutionary War, carried it with him to England and ultimately placed it in the Fulham Library. Hutchinson was a scholar, a collector of historical material, and the author of a singularly impartial History of Massachusetts. If this conjecture be true, it is clear that the property in the manuscript never could have been changed by this transaction.

The only other plausible conjecture concerning the transfer of the manuscript to Fulham is that it may have been carried off by the British army under Sir William Howe, or by some person who left Boston in their company, when that town was evacuated in March, 1776. The Old South Church had been taken possession of by the soldiers and used as a riding-school. The Prince Library was at that time in a room in the church tower. It is possible that some curious officer took possession of the manuscript and carried it home with him. But in that way no title to it by conquest, or as booty, or prize of war, could have been gained. Boston was never hostile territory to the English army before its evacuation. It was in the possession of the royal troops, and the royal authority over it was undisturbed until March 16th, 1776, the day of the evacuation; although the rebels possessed the surrounding country and besieged the town. The independence of the United States was not declared until the Fourth of July, 1776. So the case is the same as if during the English Rebellion some rebel forces had besieged Oxford or Cambridge, and compelled the King's troops to evacuate the place. Surely any book or manuscript which might have been carried off from the University Library by any member of the evacuating force would not be deemed to have changed ownership if it had been afterward deposited at Fulham.

If, however, the manuscript be treated as mere booty, we are not disposed, for the purpose of this application, to deny that in such case the property would have passed in accordance with the strict law of war. But we confidently submit to your Lordship that no civilized nation, least of all so enlightened and liberal a nation as Great Britain, would in modern times avail itself of that principle in dealing with the property of libraries, universities, or other seminaries of education. There are several interesting precedents bearing upon this matter. These precedents show that in the bloodiest and angriest wars such property is respected as forming an exception to the severe rights of warfare, and is entitled to protection. When the possession of such property has been changed by military operations, the conqueror has hastened to restore it. The Government of the United States in its "Instructions for the Government of Armies in the Field," originally prepared by Dr. Lieber, revised by a board of officers of which Major-General Hitchcock was President, and approved by President Lincoln in 1863, binds itself by this rule.

We are told that the Emperor of Russia has recently given a conspicuous example of respect for this principle by ordering the restoration of property belonging to a public library captured by his troops.

But we prefer in this matter to rest upon the precedents

established by England herself, who has so often set to mankind an example of justice and moderation in the enforcement of the laws of war.

During our War of Independence, the buildings of the college of William and Mary were repeatedly occupied by British troops. They were in every instance respected as sacred to the cause of letters, and left intact. After the close of the war, Louis XVI., the ally of America, caused the buildings, accidentally destroyed by the fire of his troops, to be replaced and every injury to be repaired.

At the occupation of Paris in 1815, the allied sovereigns rejected the principle that objects of art were legitimate spoils of war, and restored to the nations of Europe many famous statues and pictures which France had accumulated in Paris, the trophies of her wars.

In our war with Great Britain in 1812, a number of paintings and prints, designed for the Academy of Arts at Philadelphia, were captured on their passage from Italy, and taken into Halifax. Dr. Croke, the distinguished judge of the admiralty court, without hesitation, ordered them to be restored. He said, "The arts and sciences are admitted among all civilized nations as forming an exception to the severe rights of warfare, and as entitled to favor and protection. They are considered, not as the peculium of this or that nation, but as the property of mankind at large, and as belonging to the common interest of the whole species." He added, "Heaven forbid that such an application to the generosity of Great Britain should ever be ineffectual." Case of the Marquis de Someruelos, Stewart's Nova Scotia Rep., p. 482.

The British troops, under Tryon, when they occupied Yale College in 1779, spared the college buildings, although its students in arms harassed their approach. But President Clap's manuscripts were carried off. President Stiles addressed a letter to General Tryon, in which he represented that "a war against science had been reprobated for ages by the wisest and most powerful generals. The irreparable losses sustained by the Alexandrian Library and other ancient monuments of literature have prompted the victorious commanders of modern ages to exempt these monuments from the ravages and desolations inseparable to the highest rigors of war." General Tryon replied, that "disposed by principle as well as inclination to prevent the violence of war from injuring the rights of the republic of learning, he very much approved of the President's solicitude for the recovery of the manuscripts," and caused every effort to be made for their recovery and restoration.

It is, we suppose, due to this humane and benevolent principle that the ancient schools and colleges of England, whatever side they may have taken in the civil wars, have enjoyed immunity from injury, when even her stately and venerable cathedrals have not been spared. These schools and colleges have survived all changes of dynasty, all changes of institutions and manners. Puritan and Cavalier, York and Lancaster, have fought out their battles, and yet in the wildest tempest of public excitement, they

Lift not their spears against the Muses' bower.

A recent instance in our own history shows that the people of the United States are disposed to follow the example set them by their English kindred. We send you an extract from a report printed in the Bulletin of the Library Co. of Philadelphia, for July, 1867.

"In the autumn of last year the attention of the Board of Directors was called to five volumes of Manuscripts which had been presented to the Library in 1799. An examination of these volumes made it evident that they were a part of the National Archives of Great Britain. They consisted of official correspondence relating to Ireland, many of the letters bearing the sign manual of King James I. and one of Elizabeth. It was first ascertained through Mr. Hepworth Dixon, who was familiar with the State Papers preserved in the Rolls House in London, that the series of Letters of which these volumes were a part, is preserved in London in the custody of the Master of the Rolls. The directors, considering that there was an eminent propriety in the MS. being restored to the British Government as a portion of their public archives, an offer to do so was made to Lord Romilly, the Master of the Rolls. The offer was transmitted to the Lords of the Treasury, and was by them gratefully accepted." In the course of the correspondence

which ensued Lord Romilly desires "to express to the
Library Company of Philadelphia (his) deep sense
of the obligation conferred by them on the British
Nation, and (his) conviction that this, and acts of a
similar character will rivet more closely the ties of
friendship and respect which already bind our countries
together."

The following letter on this subject was received from
Sir Frederick W. A. Bruce, G. C. B., the British Minister
at Washington :

> "BRITISH LEGATION, WASHINGTON, D. C.,
> "*Feb. 27, 1867.*

> "SIR : The Master of the Rolls has brought under
the notice of the Lords Commissioners of her Majesty's
Treasury the offer made through you by the Directors
of the Library Company of Philadelphia, to restore to
the British Government a valuable and important part
of the national records of Great Britain, which have
been found in their collection.
> "I am instructed to say that the offer is gratefully
accepted by their Lordships, and it is my pleasing
duty at the same time to add that the honorable and
disinterested spirit which has prompted the gift, is
highly appreciated by her Majesty's Government."

We suppose that a thorough research would discover
many other examples of the observance of this humane
principle by civilized nations in modern times. But we do
not conceive that it is necessary to multiply instances. We
are quite sure that if there were no precedent your Lordship would be glad to establish one.

> GEORGE F. HOAR,
> STEPHEN SALISBURY,
> EDWARD EVERETT HALE,
> SAMUEL A. GREEN,
> *for the American Antiquarian*
> *Society.*

CHARLES FRANCIS ADAMS,
WILLIAM LAWRENCE,
CHARLES W. ELIOT,
for the Massachusetts Historical
Society.

ARTHUR LORD,
WILLIAM M. EVARTS,
WILLIAM T. DAVIS,
for the Pilgrim Society
of Plymouth.

CHARLES C. BEAMAN,
JOSEPH H. CHOATE,
J. PIERPONT MORGAN,
for the New England Society
of New York.

ROGER WOLCOTT,
Lieutenant Governor of
Massachusetts,
and acting Governor.

At the same time the following private letters were addressed to the Archbishop of Canterbury and the Bishop of London :—

NOVEMBER 18TH, 1896.

TO THE RIGHT REV. THE ARCHBISHOP OF CANTERBURY :

MY LORD: You will doubtless remember the brief conversation I had with you at Fulham on the twenty-second of September last, in which I expressed a strong desire for the restoration to Massachusetts of the manuscript of Gov. William Bradford's History. This is to Americans the most precious relic of the kind in existence. It contains the history of the gathering of the Pilgrim company in Lincolnshire and Yorkshire, their life for thirteen years in Holland, the voyage of the Mayflower, and the Pilgrim State at Plymouth for its first twenty-eight years. You were good enough to say that while you had not known

4

before how highly this manuscript is esteemed by Americans, that if it had depended on you it would have gone back to America long ago. You said further that before taking action you should deem it proper to consult the Archbishop of Canterbury, and that you thought the permission of the Queen should be obtained.

A communication has been sent to the present Bishop of London, signed by representatives of two of our most distinguished historical societies and of the Pilgrim Society of Plymouth and of the New England Society of New York and by Governor Wolcott, the present acting Governor of Massachusetts, of which State the old Plymouth now forms a part. I have not felt at liberty to quote the conversation I had with you in this connection because I was not sure that I was at liberty to repeat it, and because, also, I supposed you would prefer to state your own opinion on such a question to having anybody undertake to state it for you. But I shall be much obliged to you if I am right in my understanding of what you said, and you remain on further reflection of the same way of thinking, if you will make your opinion known to your successor.

I have a very pleasant memory of my brief visit at Fulham, as also of the few days spent at Mr. Grenfell's delightful home on the Thames.

I am, with high regard,

Faithfully yours,

GEO. F. HOAR.

I enclose a copy of the application to the Bishop of London. Mr. Bayard, the American Ambassador, will forward it and will doubtless state the title to respect and confidence of the gentlemen who sign it.

NOVEMBER 18TH, 1896.

THE RIGHT REVEREND THE BISHOP OF LONDON:

MY LORD: I had the honor, last September, of a brief conversation with your predecessor, now the Archbishop of Canterbury, in regard to the restoration to Massachusetts of the manuscript of Bradford's History, now in the Library at Fulham. It was understood that when I got back to the United States a formal application for the restoration of this manuscript should be made to the Bishop. I will not undertake to state the conversation because I suppose his Lordship will prefer to make known his opinion for himself, if he deem proper to express it, rather than to have it repeated at second hand.

One thing has occurred to me to say in addition to what is said in the more formal letter which will be forwarded by the American Ambassador. It may be that your Lordship would hesitate about disposing of a manuscript which is the property of the Bishop's Library, and so held by you in a public and fiduciary, and not a private capacity, without an Act of Parliament, or some authority other than you have, and I suppose this hesitation would be entirely reasonable. But if you should be satisfied that the manuscript is not the property of the Library but has found its way there by some mistake or accident, I suppose you would have the authority to deal with that question without requiring the approval of anybody else. If a book belonging to the British Museum were found at Fulham, even if it had been there a hundred years, I presume you would direct its restoration, without asking anybody's leave, with as much promptness, if the case were clear, as if any visitor left his cane or umbrella in the Library by accident. But of all this you are much the most competent judge.

I am, with highest respect,

Faithfully yours,

GEO. F. HOAR.

It is to be observed, that the reprint of the History made by the Massachusetts Historical Society under the direction of Mr. Deane does not contain the very important entry which is found on the fly-leaf following that copied in our letter, viz. :

> "But Major Bradford tells me & assures me that he only lent the book of his Grandfather's to Mr. Sewall & that it being of his Grandfather's own handwriting He had so high a value for it that he would never part with ye property, but would lend it to me & desired me to get it, which I did, and write down this, that so Major Bradford and his Heirs may be known to be the right owners."

The entry of June 4, 1728, standing alone, would seem to afford strong ground for believing that it was the intent of Major Bradford to give the manuscript to the New England Library known as the Prince Library. It is true that Prince speaks of the desire to which Major Bradford assented as a desire of "lodging" this history in the New England Library. But the stipulation that Major Bradford might have the perusal of it while he lived would seem to imply that it was expected that the title would pass. Otherwise the stipulation would be unnecessary and of no effect. So the letter to the Bishop stated that "these inscriptions seem to make it clear that the manuscript belongs to the Prince Library." But the inscription on the next leaf, overlooked by the person who made the copy for the publication by the Historical Society, seems to have been made for the purpose of preventing any inference that the property in the manuscript passed by the transaction. It is further to be observed that the book-plate which follows the first entry, which reads as follows:

THIS BOOK BELONGS TO
THE NEW ENGLAND LIBRARY
BEGUN TO BE COLLECTED BY THOMAS PRINCE
UPON HIS ENTERING HARVARD COLLEGE, JULY 6
1703; AND WAS GIVEN BY.

is not filled out. Mr. Winsor, who formerly had the custody of the Prince Library in his official capacity as Librarian of the Boston Public Library, says:

"The Bradford manuscript has in it the book-plate of the Prince Library, and though there is doubt whether it was placed there by Prince or by the deacons of the Old South Church, the fact that it is not filled out in writing as Prince was in the habit of doing when he himself inserted the plates, may not bar the claim of the Boston Public Library to possess the treasure, as a representative of the deacons, on the plea that the affixing of the plate is prima facie evidence of the surrender at that time of the claim of the Bradford heirs. There is strong reason to believe that the plate was not put in by Prince.

"There are in Prince's hand some memoranda on the fly-leaves of the manuscript which acknowledge that on June 4, 1728, it came into his hands for use only, and that Major John Bradford, the grandson of Governor Bradford, and from whom he had received it, had not parted with property in the book. There is, moreover, in another note, a distinct averment that 'Major Bradford and his heirs' are the 'right owners' of it. This raises the question of moral if not legal ownership, involving the application of the law of limitations."

Taking the two entries together, it would seem that all that can be inferred from them is that the manuscript was once in the possession of the Prince Library with the consent of Major Bradford, the owner. He consented that the history should be "lodged" there. Prince uses the word "lodged," not "given" in his request. That ordinarily implies a temporary and not a permanent possession, or, to take Webster's definition, "to furnish with a temporary habitation; to provide with a transient abiding-place." All that there is on the other side is the language of Prince that Major Bradford provided that he might have the perusal of it while he lived. It may be said with great force, that he would have had no occasion to make such a stipulation unless he parted with the property. But, on the other hand, it is not unlikely that an expression of his expectation to use it might be inserted even if he were only loaning it. At any rate, as matter of legal evidence, such an entry by Prince would not be received to show title. His entry might be evidence against himself, but he could not destroy the property of the owner of the book by writing in it anything in disparagement of the title.

It would seem, then, that the trustees of the Old South Church merely had it for safe-keeping. If that were the

trust on which they had it, it would further seem that they
were not very faithful trustees. If they let Hutchinson
take it in 1767 and keep it seven years, or if they let it
stay, during the stormy times of the Revolution, in the
tower of the Old South Church to be looted by British
soldiers, they were not very faithful to their trust. If,
when its existence at Fulham was discovered in 1856, they
heard of it, as undoubtedly they must have heard of it,
they neglected to assert their legal title, or to take any
legal proceedings to get it back for forty-one years. Our
late associate, Mr. Hamilton A. Hill, in his History of the
Old South Church, Vol. 2, p. 44, states that the Prince
Library suffered from neglect and from want of appreciation of its custodians of its intrinsic value.

In the Introduction to the Catalogue of the Prince
Library, published by the trustees in 1870, is this statement :

> "The books and papers were deposited on shelves
> and in boxes and barrels in a room in the steeple of
> the church, under the belfry, which according to tradi-
> tion, had been Prince's study. There this valuable
> deposit was left for many years without care, and sub-
> ject to many vicissitudes. During the siege of Boston
> in 1775–6, the Church, being used as a riding-school
> by the British troops, was often frequented by idle
> spectators, who must have had access to the collection,
> and may be responsible for some of the loss it has
> sustained."

The Introduction to the Catalogue further expresses the
hope that "these waifs" may be returned to be forever
kept where, if they do not absolutely belong, they can be
most properly retained. This would seem to imply a good
deal of doubt whether the manuscript belonged to the
Prince Library, or to imply the suggestion that it ought to
be returned to some other custody than theirs. It is a
little curious that in the Introduction, the words "now
lodged" are used as describing the possession of the Bishop

of London ; which is precisely the expression of Prince in describing the possession of the Prince Library.

It is also a singular coincidence that Winthrop's Journal, which bears somewhat the same relation to Massachusetts that Bradford's History does to Plymouth, got into the Prince Library under circumstances which led Mr. Winthrop to believe that the volumes were borrowed from the family and never were really a part of the Library.

Another singular fact is stated in the Introduction, that so many of the books which have the book-plate of the New England Library, are found scattered about the country, and the author of the Introduction says, "It has been suggested that Prince possibly made another collection which he sold."

It is also a very striking circumstance that there is in the possession of the Massachusetts Historical Society a catalogue of the books and tracts collected by Thomas Prince, in Prince's own handwriting, made certainly as late as 1750, in which the Bradford manuscript is not included.

The decree of the Consistory Court commits the manuscript to the Governor of Massachusetts on the condition, among others, that it shall be deposited for permanent safekeeping in the archives of the Commonwealth of Massachusetts, or with the Massachusetts Historical Society. This condition the Governor has undertaken to fulfil. If, for any reason, it could not be accomplished, the Commonwealth would have been bound in honor to restore the document to the Bishop.

The Bishop, it is understood, came to the conclusion that he would not be justified in restoring the manuscript, of himself, without some legislative authority or judicial proceeding. He was, at first, inclined to seek permission from Parliament and was inclined to introduce a bill into Parliament for that purpose himself. On further consideration, it was thought better to obtain a decree of the Consistory Court of London.   Accordingly, the proceedings, copies of which are given, were had.

The observations of the judge of the Consistory Court as to the application of Mr. Henry White, Secretary to the American Embassy, require a few words of explanation in order that there may be no misunderstanding as to Mr. White's position, which does not seem to have been fully comprehended by the Court.

The *London Times* of March 26, 1897, the day after announcement of the judgment, contained, among its regular court reports, what purported to be the report of the proceedings of the Consistory Court of London, headed:

THE CONSISTORY COURT OF LONDON
BEFORE DR. TRISTRAM, Q. C.
CHANCELLOR OF THE DIOCESE OF LONDON.

It is headed:

"A sitting of the Consistory Court of London was held today in St. Paul's Cathedral before Dr. Tristram, Q. C., Chancellor of the Diocese of London, who was attended by Mr. Hugh Lee, Registrar.

"THE LOG OF THE MAYFLOWER.

"This was a petition by the Hon. Thomas F. Bayard, American Ambassador, petitioning for and on behalf of the President and citizens of the United States of America for an order of the Consistory Court of London directing that a certain manuscript book, viz: the Log of the Mayflower, which has been for many years past and is now deposited in the Library attached to Fulham Palace, might be transmitted to the President and citizens of the United States of America as one of the earliest records of their national history."

After giving the arguments on both sides and the testimony of Mr. Harry W. Lee, there follows what purports to be a verbatim report of the judgment or decree, which closes by saying:

"The Court makes a decree for the transmission of this manuscript back to the President and Senate of the United States of America, subject to certain terms and conditions which I will settle in Chambers."

The newspapers, at or about the same date, reported that Mr. Bayard had gone on a journey to Italy. There was no statement as to the length of his journey. It seemed not unlikely that he might be intending to take a journey which would occupy the entire summer. Under these circumstances the decree of the court excited some consternation. It had been hoped that the document might be received in Massachusetts in time for the meeting of the American Antiquarian Society, which was to take place April 21st, but at any rate in time to be presented to the Governor of Massachusetts before the adjournment of the Legislature, so that any arrangements for its reception and safe-keeping which should require legislation might be made. The order in the decree that the document should be transmitted to the President and Senate was practically incapable of execution. There was no way known to our constitutional proceeding by which the President and Senate could jointly take custody of such a document. The original petition addressed to the Bishop by the societies, as will be seen, prayed "that your Lordship direct that it be given to the American Ambassador to be by him restored to Massachusetts." The custody of the document at the seat of government in Washington would be hardly more convenient or satisfactory than its remaining at Fulham. It became necessary, therefore, if this decree were to stand, to get an order from the President and Senate, if possible, before the adjournment of Congress, directing the transmission of the manuscript to Massachusetts according to the original prayer.

Mr. Hay had been appointed Ambassador, and Mr. Bayard's letter of recall had been presented. Mr. Hay's credentials could not be presented until the return of Her

Majesty from the Continent and, according to custom, it was not expected that he would appear in public in England until he had been received. So he still remained in Washington. The embassy, in the meantime, was to be in charge of Mr. White, the Secretary. He had gone to New York to take the steamer for England when the news of the decree and of Mr. Bayard's departure for the Continent came. Accordingly, the writer addressed at once a letter to Mr. White asking him, as soon as he reached London, to apply for the delivery of the manuscript to him in order that it might be received here before the adjournment of the Legislature and, if possible, in time for the meeting of the Antiquarian Society on the 21st of April. He very kindly made the request, not, as the Chancellor erroneously recites, in behalf of Mr. Hay, who had not then entered upon his office, but in his own behalf, as Chargé ad interim. There was no desire on the part of anybody to deprive Mr. Bayard of the opportunity of bringing the document back according to the desire expressed in the original petition to the Bishop. But the difficulty grew out, first, of the uncertainty on this side as to the time of Mr. Bayard's return from the Continent, and second, from the mistake of the judge himself in making the order, practically impossible of execution and never contemplated by the promoters of the application, that the document should be given to the President and Senate,—an order made without familiarity with our constitutional arrangements here.

Here follow copies of the further correspondence as to the matter and of the records of the Consistory Court.

JANUARY 7, 1897.

DEAR MR. OLNEY :

There is a strong desire felt to have the original manuscript of Governor Bradford's History of Plymouth restored to Massachusetts. An application to that effect has been signed by myself, Mr. Salisbury, and Dr. Samuel A. Green, for the Antiquarian Society ; Charles Francis Adams, Bishop Lawrence, and President Eliot, for the Historical Society ; Arthur Lord, William M. Evarts, and William T. Davis, for the Pilgrim Society ; and Charles C. Beaman, Joseph H. Choate, and J. Pierpont Morgan, for the New England Society of New York.

I spoke to Mr. Bayard about the matter when I was in London. He took great interest in it, and kindly undertook to do whatever he properly might to promote the application.

I enclose a copy of the letter to the Bishop of London which tells the whole story. I think you will find it interesting.

If the rules and practice of your Department permit, will you kindly say a word to Mr. Bayard, expressing your interest in the matter and your hope that it may be accomplished. I suppose I can hardly ask you to do this in any formal or official way. But if Mr. Bayard have the right to say that the success of the application will gratify you, or the President, I presume it would help the matter.

If there be no objection, I should like to send the documents in the Government despatch bag.

I am, with high regard, faithfully yours,

GEO. F. HOAR.

The Honorable
    RICHARD OLNEY,
        Secretary of State, etc., etc., etc.

DEPARTMENT OF STATE.

WASHINGTON, *January 8, 1897.*

Hon. GEORGE F. HOAR, *United States Senate.*

SIR : I have the honor to acknowledge the receipt of your very interesting letter of yesterday with accompanying papers, relative to the application of the American Antiquarian Society, the Massachusetts Historical Society, the Pilgrim Society of Plymouth, the New England Society of New York and the Governor of the Commonwealth of Massachusetts to the Right Reverend the Bishop of London, calling the attention of His Lordship to the original manuscript of Governor Bradford's History of Plymouth now in the library at Fulham, and asking that that document may be delivered to the United States Ambassador at London to be by him restored to the State of Massachusetts.

In reply I beg to inform you that it has afforded me much pleasure to cause, in accordance with your request, the above mentioned papers to be sent in the despatch bag to the United States Embassy at London, with instructions to Mr. Bayard to informally bring the matter in question to the attention of the Bishop of London with a view to obtaining the restoration of the Bradford manuscript to the State of Massachusetts.

Adding that the Ambassador's reply will be promptly communicated to you,

I have the honor to be, Sir,

Your obedient servant,

RICHARD OLNEY.

DEPARTMENT OF STATE.

WASHINGTON, *January 12, 1897.*

Hon. GEORGE F. HOAR, *United States Senate.*

SIR: Referring to previous correspondence relative to instructions to the United States Ambassador at London in regard to making application for the State of Massachusetts to the Bishop of London for the original manuscript of Governor Bradford's History of Plymouth, now in the library at Fulham, I have the honor to acknowledge the receipt of your letter of the 9th instant, transmitting a parcel containing papers relating to the subject which you desire to have sent to the United States Ambassador at London.

In reply I have to inform you that the parcel in question will at once be sent to its destination with suitable instructions.

I have the honor to be, Sir,

Your obedient servant,

RICHARD OLNEY.

EMBASSY OF THE UNITED STATES.

LONDON, *January 18, 1897.*

MY DEAR LORD BISHOP:

You have doubtless received a communication from Worcester in Massachusetts, written on behalf of the American Antiquarian Society, the Massachusetts Historical Society, the Pilgrim Society of Plymouth and the New England Society of New York, and with the approval of the Governor of that Commonwealth, in relation to the restoration to Massachusetts of the MS. history of that Commonwealth, written there, in the 17th century, by William Bradford, the Second Governor of Plymouth Colony, as appears by the inscription on the fly-leaf of the document, which is now in the library at Fulham Palace, where it was deposited after the breaking out of the war of the American Revolution.

The letter so addressed to you, fully and forcibly sets forth the strong and very natural desire felt in the United States to have a document, so clearly and solely connected with the early history of the original settlement of that country, restored to the descendants of those settlers in the locality in which the events occurred.

The Secretary of State of the United States has requested me informally to bring the subject to your attention. And I am sure that I represent the strong desire of my countrymen, in asking that I may be allowed, in a personal interview (whenever and wherever it will be most convenient to you) to state the great interest felt in Massachusetts in the matter, and to express my belief that the gratification of the earnest wishes of my countrymen would be a sensible addition to the sentiments of amity, sympathy and respect between the two great branches of the English-speaking race, which it is my high honour to advocate.

It is my impression that the Hon. George F. Hoar, a Senator in Congress from Massachusetts, held communication with your predecessor (now the Archbishop of Canterbury) on this interesting subject and, as I remember, was encouraged to hope that means would be found to accom-

plish the restoration of the MS., written in America, and
of America, to the custody and possession of Americans.

Believe me, &c.,

(sd) T. F. BAYARD.

The Right Hon. and Right Rev.

MANDELL CREIGHTON, D.D.,

Bishop of London.

(Copy.)

EMBASSY OF THE UNITED STATES.

LONDON, *January 23, 1897.*

MY DEAR LORD BISHOP:

It will give me great pleasure to have a little conversation with you respecting the William Bradford MS., which is now in the Fulham Library, and is so ardently desired by the Commonwealth of Massachusetts, as part of their early history by the hand of their second Governor. In accordance with your kind suggestion I will be most happy to see you at 5 p. m. on Wednesday next (the 27th) at my residence, 83 Eaton Square.

I enclose herewith an imprint of the letter to your Lordship from the Committee representing the Petitioners for the restoration of the MS., which you tell me you have not yet received, and will acquaint you with their wishes regarding the MS. in question.

And I am, &c.,

(sd) T. F. BAYARD.

The Right Hon. and Right Rev.

Bishop of London,

Deanery, St. Paul's.

(Unofficial.)

EMBASSY OF THE UNITED STATES.

123 VICTORIA ST., S. W.

LONDON, *January 28, 1897.*

DEAR MR. HOAR:

Your missives through the State Department in relation to obtaining the MS. of Governor William Bradford came safely, and had my immediate and friendly attention.

Yesterday afternoon the Bishop of London, Dr. Mandell Creighton, came pursuant to our arrangement, to my residence, and in his hands I placed the letters, imprinted and written, to the Archbishop of Canterbury, and those addressed to himself. He is most favorably disposed, and I am satisfied is anxious to promote the restoration of the MS. to Massachusetts. The result of our interview was his promise to communicate with the Marquis of Salisbury, after which he will write me on the subject. He suggested that action by Parliament might be necessary, and that a bill to effectuate the transfer could be introduced by himself in the House of Lords.

I dwelt upon the very good effect internationally of the return of the MS. of Bradford in which view he promptly concurred, and spoke with great kindness of Harvard and its officers. He was, as you may remember, the representative of John Harvard's college (St. John was it not?) at the 250th commemoration at Cambridge in Massachusetts in 1887. I enclose copies of the notes I addressed to the Bishop of London, in order to let you see the progress of the case in which you feel so great an interest, and so soon as I hear again from Bishop Creighton, I will again write to you.

Believe me

Very truly,

T. F. BAYARD.

Hon. G. F. Hoar, U. S. S.

(Personal.)

EMBASSY OF THE UNITED STATES.

London, *March 17, 1897.*

Dear Mr. Hoar:

I have just seen the Bishop of London, and believe I can speak most hopefully of the early delivery to me, as intermediary for the Commonwealth of Massachusetts, of the MS. history of the Colony of Massachusetts Bay by Governor William Bradford.

I am sure you will not care for the absence of technicalities in the arrangements that have for their termination the

delivery of the MS. into the hands of Massachusetts.
When we meet I can explain to you what has transpired
here and the reason why the authorities here prefer *in
their own way* to gratify the wishes which were the basis
of our correspondence.

In a few days I expect a communication from the Bishop
of London, and will lose no time in letting you know the
conclusion arrived at, which as I have said, I fully expect
to be favorable to your wishes.

Believe me

Sincerely yours,

T. F. BAYARD.

Hon. GEORGE F. HOAR, *U. S. Senate.*

19 DOVER STREET, *May 3, 1897.*

DEAR MR. HOAR:

On last Thursday, the Chancellor of the Episcopal and
Consistorial Court of London delivered his final decision,
sustaining his prior decree, in March, for the manual
delivery, on my petition, of the log of the "Mayflower,"
and complying with the terms of his order. I paid the
costs, gave my receipt for the MS. book, and the precious
volume was placed personally in my hands by the Bishop
of London.

I mailed you a copy of the "Times" with a full report
of the proceedings, and wrote to Governor Wolcott notify-
ing him of the facts, and that I expected to embark from
Southampton on the 8th inst. for New York with the book
in my possession, and would in obedience to the decree,
and to my written obligation deliver the document and
original decree to him in Boston as soon as practicable
after my arrival, and I also enclosed a copy of the
"Times" report.

Being without clerical aid I could not send him in
advance a full copy of the decree, but I stated sufficiently
its provisions.

Nor had I time before closing of the mail to write to
you, and could only send you the "Times" report.

No doubt the telegraph informed you of the all-important

fact, that the log of the "Mayflower" was now on its way back to Massachusetts.

I have your letter of April 21st, and had arranged before my departure from London on my leave of absence for the execution of all the formalities requisite for the final action by the Bishop of London.

Happily an avoidance of some technical obstacles was accomplished, and it is with sincere satisfaction that I am now enabled to communicate the success of the efforts initiated by you last year in London to obtain possession of this pregnant historical record and its restoration to the hands of its proper custodians.

I should be delinquent in manifest duty did I not attest the spirit of amity, kinship and international courtesy exhibited by every official (civil and ecclesiastical) of this Government, having connection with this transaction, and the evident public satisfaction the incident has caused throughout this country ; and of this our countrymen should be made aware.

To no one is felicitation more due than to you personally, upon the result, and I sincerely tender it, and am

Very faithfully yours,

T. F. BAYARD.

The Hon. GEORGE F. HOAR, *U. S. Senate.*

4 AIRLIE GARDENS, CAMPDEN HILL,
LONDON, W. *January 1st, 1897.*

MY DEAR SIR, When and why Gov. Bradford's manuscript History came to be deposited in the Library of the Bishop of London, perhaps you have not yet decided, and may entertain kindly a suggestion which occurs to me.

I was much impressed by your doubts as to the usual conjecture that it was brought to London, when the British army evacuated Boston in 1776. If that had been so, the MS. would probably have been transferred to the Colonial Office, and would now be, among papers regarding old colonial affairs, in the Public Record Office.

But it is in the custody of the church, and not treated as a state paper, and may have been left there for some ecclesiastical purpose.

5

It could hardly have been among Gov. Hutchinson's
papers, destroyed by the mob in 1765, as the editor of his
last volume, his nephew, referring, in a note to the preface,
to the "many ancient records and papers" thus destroyed,
says expressly "*one*, and perhaps the most curious of these
documents, escaped, and is now in the editor's possession.
It is the original Court Book of the Colony of Massachusetts Bay, kept at first in England, and containing records
of as early a date as February, 1628." And the MS. is not
mentioned, I believe, by Hutchinson.

I have lately been reading the book (Bishop Wilberforce's History of the Episcopal Church in America) which,
by quotations from the Bradford Manuscript, gave a clue
to its discovery and publication by the Massachusetts Historical Society. Bishop Wilberforce did not quote this
manuscript alone, but also other "Fulham Mss." in his
History, and all chiefly for the purpose of showing the
long-continued endeavours and need of the Episcopalian
Churches in America to have one or more Bishops in their
own country, for the ordination of their ministers and
other wants of their Church Government, instead of being
dependent, as they were, on the distant Bishop of London :—and he says this effort was made very strongly in
the years just preceding the Revolution!

It was at this time, according to Doyle, that the MS.
was last heard of in Massachusetts, in 1767.

Is it not likely that it was sent over to the Bishop of
London as evidence of the long and difficult existence of
the Episcopal Church in America, even from the early days
of Plymouth Colony, and of its need of the more independent and strong government, which its scattered branches
in the Colonies were then trying to obtain?

Among the old letters in the Fulham Library on this
subject, it is possible that Bishop Wilberforce found the
Bradford Manuscript; he refers to it, as well as to the
letters, as "Fulham MSS.,"—and possibly in some one of
these letters may be found an explanation of the occasion
and the date of the deposit of the Bradford MS.

The efforts of the Episcopal Church in America to have
Bishops of their own were of course ended by the Revolution : and the old manuscripts on the subject of this lapsed
and terminated cause, seem hardly worth preserving at

Fulham, especially as to such an unused piece of documentary evidence as the Bradford Manuscript, while its possession as an historical document must be admitted to be of great value to Massachusetts : and perhaps the present Episcopal Bishop of Massachusetts may assist in its restoration.

As the present Archbishop of Canterbury, lately Bishop of London, received so favourably your conversation with him on the subject, and the newly appointed Bishop of London, Dr. Creighton, has a Harvard degree, and is so pre-eminently an historical student and author, I hope your application for the MS. will soon be successful, and that it will be returned to the old Commonwealth where it rightly belongs.

I am, very sincerely yours,

JOSIAH PIERCE.

Hon. GEORGE F. HOAR.

In the Consistory Court of London.

PETITION OF THE HON. T. F. BAYARD.

To The Worshipful Thomas Hutchinson Tristram Doctor of Laws, Vicar General of The Right Honorable and Right Reverend Mandell by Divine Permission Lord Bishop of London and Official Principal of the Consistorial and Episcopal Court of London lawfully constituted, his Surrogate or some other competent Judge in this behalf.

The humble Petition of The Honorable Thomas F. Bayard (Ambassador Extraordinary and Plenipotentiary in London of the United States of America) for and on behalf of the President and Citizens of the said States

SHEWETH, That there is in the Custody of the said Lord Bishop of the Diocese of London a manuscript book containing an account as narrated by one of the company of Englishmen who left England in April in the year 1620 in the Ship known as the "Mayflower" of the circumstances leading to the prior settlement of that Company at Leyden in Holland their return to England and subsequent departure for New England their landing at Cape Cod December 1620 settlement at New Plymouth and later history for several years, they being the Company whose settlement

in America is regarded as the first real colonisation of the
New England States.

That on the second page of the Book is a statement in
the handwriting of Samuel Bradford, a Grandson of
William Bradford who was one of the voyagers in the
"Mayflower" and the second Governor of the newly settled
Community of 1620 to the effect that such manuscript
book was written by his Grandfather and a further statement on pages 3 and 4 by one Thomas Prince that the
book had been loaned to him by Major John Bradford in
1728 but that the right and property therein attached to
the said John Bradford. A printed ticket therein is to
the effect that the book belonged to a certain New England
Library begun to be collected by the said Thomas Prince
but there is no evidence of how the Book was placed at
his disposal for this purpose nor is there any evidence to
shew how as stated on such printed Ticket "it came to be
deposited in the Bishop of London's Library at Fulham."

That the said Manuscript Book has been for many years
past and is now deposited in the Library attached to
Fulham Palace.

That the said Manuscript Book is of the greatest interest
importance and value to the Citizens of the United States
of America inasmuch as it is one of the earliest records of
their National History and contains much valuable information in regard to the Original Settlers in the States, their
family history and antecedents and therefore your Petitioner
earnestly desires to acquire possession of the same for and
on behalf of the President and Citizens of the said United
States of America.

That your Petitioner is informed that the said Right
Honorable and Right Reverend Mandell Lord Bishop of
London fully recognises the value and interest of the said
manuscript book to the Citizens of the United States and
the claims which they have to its possession and that he is
desirous of transferring it to the said President and Citizens.

That your Petitioner is advised and believes that the
Custody of documents in the nature of public or ecclesiasti-
cal record belonging to the See of London is vested in the
Consistorial Court of the said See and that any disposal
thereof must be authorized by an Order issued by the
Judge of this Honorable Court.

Your Petitioner therefore humbly prays that this Honorable Court will deliver to your Petitioner the said Manuscript Book before referred to your Petitioner undertaking to use every means in his power for the safe transmission of the said book to the United States of America and its secure deposit and custody in the Pilgrim Hall at New Plymouth or in such other place as may be selected by the President and Senate of the said United States and upon such other conditions as to security and access by and on behalf of the English Nation as this Honorable Court may determine.

HARRY W. LEE,
Att'y for the Petitioner.

I concur in this Petition,

M. LONDON.

22 March 1897.

In the Consistory Court of London.

IN THE MATTER OF AN APPLICATION FOR AN ORDER FOR DELIVERY OF THE MANUSCRIPT "MAYFLOWER" LOG TO THE AMERICAN AMBASSADOR.

AFFIDAVIT OF HARRY W. LEE, ESQ.

In the Consistory Court of London.

IN THE MATTER OF AN APPLICATION FOR AN ORDER FOR THE DELIVERY OF THE MANUSCRIPT "MAYFLOWER" LOG TO THE AMERICAN AMBASSADOR.

I Harry Wilmot Lee of No. 1 The Sanctuary in the City of Westminster make oath and say as follows:

1 I am legal Secretary to the Right Reverend Mandell by Divine Permission Lord Bishop of London.

2 The Petition dated twenty second March 1897 made by me acting for and on behalf of The Honorable Thomas F. Bayard for delivery to him of the manuscript book before referred to which Petition is now produced to me and is marked with the letter "A" is to the best of my knowledge and belief true in every particular.

3 It is within my knowledge that the said Lord
Bishop consents to the handing over of the manuscript
book referred to in the said Petition upon such conditions as shall be deemed proper by the Judge of the
Consistory Court of the Diocese of London.

Sworn at 1 The Sanctuary in the ⎫
City of Westminster this 22ⁿᵈ day ⎪
of March 1897, Before me, ⎪
  HENRY L. BOLTON,   HARRY W. LEE.
A Commissioner to administer Oaths ⎪
in the Supreme Court of Judicature ⎪
in England. ⎭

In the Consistory Court of London.

IN RE THE MATTER OF "THE LOG OF THE MAYFLOWER."

NOTES OF EVIDENCE GIVEN AT THE APPLICATION.

In the Consistory Court of London.

RE THE MATTER OF "THE LOG OF THE MAYFLOWER."

NOTES OF EVIDENCE.

The Application of Harry Wilmot Lee.

I am Legal Secretary to the present Bishop of London.
I was joint Legal Secretary to his Lordship's Predecessors,
Bishop Tait, Bishop Jackson & for a time to Bishop
Temple, & afterwards I was his Sole Legal Secretary. I
am Solicitor in this Case for Mr. Bayard the present American Ambassador at the Court of St. James. He instructed
me to file a Petition on behalf of the President and Citizens of the United States praying that the Log of the
Mayflower should be delivered over to him for the purpose
of his conveying it in safety to the United States & of
its being placed in public custody in the City of Boston in
the United States Mr. Bayard will give an undertaking,
that he will take every care of it during its transmission to
The States & on its arrival there will himself convey it to
the Governor of Massachusetts & deposit it in his custody.
The Lord Bishop of London concurs in the prayer of the
Petition, and has attached his signature to a Memorandum
at the end of it signifying his concurrence in it. I have
inspected this original Manuscript. I produce a Fac Simile

Photograph Copy of it published by Messrs Ward & Downey in London.

The Photographic Copy was prepared under the care of M^r. Boyle, Fellow of All Souls College, Oxford, and Printed by Spottiswood.

Two Duplicate Copies of this Manuscript will be furnished by Mr. Bayard, one for the purpose of its being placed in the Fulham Palace Library and the other in the Bishop of London's Registry in Doctor's Commons.

> The American Antiquarian Society,
> The Historical Society of Massachusetts,
> The Pilgrim's Society at Plymouth,
> The New England Society of New York,

acting with the Co-operation of the Governor of the Commonwealth of Massachusetts are all desirous that this Manuscript should be transferred to Boston & there placed in Public Custody.

I have been Legal Secretary to the Bishops of London for from 20 to 25 years. There is a Muniment Room over the Gateway of Fulham Palace with which I am acquainted & in which I have made searches for Documents of importance. I have reason to believe it contains correspondence relating to the American Church prior to the Declaration of Independence. It is the Palace Muniment Room, I got the papers from there which enabled Col. Maitland to establish his claim to the Earldom of Laudersdale before the House of Lords. There is a Register of the Papers there but not a complete one.

In the House of Lords in this Case these documents were held to have come from a Public Registry & were on this ground admitted in evidence. The present Bishop of London directed this Book to be placed in the Registry here temporarily. He considers the Fulham Muniment Room an adjunct to the Bishop of London's Registry in Doctors Commons.

Cur Adv Vult.

In the Consistory Court of London.

IN THE MATTER OF THE LOG OF THE MAYFLOWER.

Judgment delivered at St. Paul's Cathedral on March 25, 1897.

IN THE MATTER OF THE LOG OF THE MAYFLOWER.

The Honble Thomas F. Bayard the Ambassador Extraordinary of the United States of America to the Court of S^t. James has petitioned this Court on behalf of the President and Citizens of the United States of America to decree that an Original Manuscript Book known as "The Log of The Mayflower" in the Custody of the Court be delivered to his Excellency for safe transmission to the President and Senate of the United States upon such conditions and security as the Court may determine.

This Manuscript Book (amongst other matters of great historical interest) contains what in law is an authentic Register between 1620 & 1650 of the Names of the persons who founded in 1620 the Colony of New England in North America, of the fact of their Marriages, with the names of their respective wives, & of their children, the lawful issue of such Marriages, & of the Marriages of many of their grand-children, & of the issue of such Marriages, as well as the deaths of persons therein named. It is in its character of being an authentic Register of Marriages, Births, & Deaths of persons resident in a Territory which formed part of the Colonial Possessions of Great Britain, at the dates of which they relate, & which was by custom then within the Diocese of London, that the Custody of this Manuscript belongs to the Court.

The authenticity of the Manuscript as being, (with the exception of the four last entries on the last page) in the handwriting of Major William Bradford, one of the Founders, & the second Governor of the Colony is placed beyond doubt, from the inherent evidence furnished by its contents, & by the fact of the whole of the contents, with the above exceptions, being in his handwriting, as well as by an entry prefixed to it in the handwriting of his grandson Samuel Bradford. The following headnote in Major Bradford's handwriting is prefixed to the Register, which is contained in the last 5 pages of the Book.

"The Names of those which came over first in 1620, and "were (by the Blessing of God) the first beginners and

" (in a sort,) the foundation of all the Plantations & Colo-
"nies in New England & their families."

Then follow twenty seven separate entries, each containing the name of the head of each Emigrant Family, and
the names of his wife, children & Servants who accompanied him on the voyage of The Mayflower or who subsequently joined him at Plymouth.

At the End of these entries comes this entry.

"These being about 100 souls come over in this first
"Ship, & began this work which God of His Goodness
"hath hitherto blessed ; let his Holy Name have the praise,
"and seeing it hath pleased him to give me to see 30 years
"completed since these beginnings, & that the Great works
"of This Providence are to be observed, I have thought it
"not unworthy my paines to take a view of the decreasings
"& increasings of these persons, & such changes as has
"passed over them and theirs in this 30 years—It may be
"some use to such as come after. I will therefore take
"them in order as they lye"—Then follow entries of the
Marriages, Births & Deaths of the surviving families of the
Settlers, accompanied with notices relating to some of them.

The Writer then proceeds : —"Of these 100 persons
"which came first over, in this first ship—the greater part
"dyed in the general mortality ; & most of them in 2 or 3
"months time, & for those who survived, though some
"were ancient & past procreation & others left the place &
"country, yet of those few remains are sprung up 100
"persons in this 30 years, & are now living in this present
"year 1650, besides many of their children which are dead,
"& come not within this account. And of the oldest
"(stock of one or other) there are yet living this present
"year 1650 near 30 persons—Let the Lord have the praise,
"who is the High Preserver of them."

The entry prefixed to the Book by Major Bradford's
Grandson is as follows : —"This Book was writ by my
"Grandfather William Bradford, & given to his Son Major
"William Bradford, & by him to his Son Major John
"Bradford."

" Writ by me Samuel Bradford "
"March 20, 1705 "

Then follows the Signature

John Bradford.

There is an Entry on the next page but one—
March 20   Samuel Bradford
" But Major Bradford tells me & assures me that he only
" lent this Book of his Grandfather to M.ʳ Sewell, & it
" being of his Grandfather's own writing he had so high a
" value for it, that he would never part with the property,
" but would lend it to me, & desired me to get it which I
" did, & write down this that so Major Bradford & his heirs
" may be known to be the right owners—Written when the
" Book came into my hands."
    Then comes the following Entry on the previous page—
" This Book belongs to the New England Library."
    " Begun to be collected by Thos : Prince upon his enter-
ing Harvard College July 6. 1703 & was given by
    It now belongs to the Bishop of London's Library at
" Fulham."
    The History of Major Bradford as bearing on the authen-
ticity & legal authority of this Register is, that he arrived
at Plymouth in New England in the Mayflower in December 1620, that in April 1621—Carver the Governor of
Plymouth died & Bradford was elected to fill the vacancy
in the Governorship occasioned by Carver's death, that he
resigned the Governorship in 1633—was re-elected in 1635
—and retained it until 1650—when he resigned it, & died
on May 9 1657, aged 67 & that during all this period up
to 1650 his high Official position as Governor was recognised from the entries in the Manuscript by the Sovereigns
of this Country.
    These entries in the Register having been officially
recorded by the highest Officer of State in the Colony are
entitled to be admitted as evidence in Courts of Justice,
in Pedigree Cases, of the facts therein recorded.
    No record or evidence has been found as to how or at
what date this Manuscript Book came into the Custody of
the Bishops of London.
    From the Entries in the Book it is clear that M.ʳ Prince
was anxious for securing permanent possession of it for
the Library he had established in Massachusetts & that the
Bradford Family had determined to retain it in their possession.   It must have been deposited at Fulham Palace
after 1727 & before the Declaration of the Independence
of the States of America.   The most probable grounds of

its being placed there would be that up to the time of the Declaration of Independence New England was for Ecclesiastical purposes in the Diocese of London, & that it has been the practice to transmit from the Colonies & from Foreign parts Certificates of the Marriages, Births & Deaths of British Subjects to the Bishop of London's Registry for safe custody & reference in this Country; the Bishops Registry being the only Public Registry for the Custody of such documents within the Diocese & from the circumstance of the whole manuscript with the exception of the last five pages being of historical interest the Register at the end of it might have been overlooked & thus it was retained amongst the other Historical Documents connected with the North American Colonies in the Episcopal Registry at Fulham Palace simply as a Historical Manuscript.

On M^r. Bayard making application to the Bishop of London to allow this Document to be transmitted to the President & Senate of the United States for custody it appeared to his Lordship after enquiries as to the practice of the Diocese in such Cases more especially on ascertaining that it contained an authentic Register of Marriages Births & Deaths which might be of importance in tracing descents and rights of succession to property, directed the Manuscript to be deposited in the Strong Room of the Registry of the Court & referred the Application to be dealt with by the Court.

The only reported Case pertinent to the present Application is in the Matter of An Application on the Motion of Her Majesty's Government to the Prerogative Court of Canterbury in 1853 for the delivery of the Original Will & Codicils of The Emperor Napoleon I, which had been proved in that Court on the 5th of August 1824 to Lord John Russell Her Majesty's Principal Secretary of State for Foreign Affairs for the purpose of being made over to the French Government upon a Notarial Copy thereof being left in the Registry of the Court. The Application was founded on an affidavit of Lord John Russell, deposing that it appeared to Her Majesty's Gov^{mt} that on grounds of public policy such application should be complied with.

The Queen's Advocate Sir John Harding referred to three cases in support of his application stating that the question was simply one of discretion; that sufficient grounds had

been set forth in the affidavit of the Secretary of State to
justify the Court in making the Decree, that no ones
interest could be injured thereby & that the surviving
Executors were consenting. In re The Will of The Emperor Napoleon Buonaparte. 2 Robertson Reports 606.
Sir John Dodson in delivering Judgment said " This is an
" Application, at the instance of the Lords of the Treasury ;
" to this Court to decree the Will & several Codicils of the
" late Napoleon Buonaparte to be delivered out of the
" Registry to Her Majesty's Principal Secretary of State
" for Foreign Affairs, for the purpose of being given up
" to the French Government. The Ground of the Applica-
" tion is stated to be public policy, which the Queen's
" Advocate seemed to think was of itself almost sufficient
" to induce the Court to grant the prayer. I cannot, how-
" ever, hold to that view ; it is necessary to show that the
" step proposed to be taken is conformable to law. Un-
" doubtedly this Court, as all other Courts, is desirous to
" carry into effect the views of Her Majesty's Government ;
" nevertheless it must not venture to go beyond the limits
" of legal authority. In a Country governed by settled
" laws, it is necessary for Courts to be guided by those
" laws, & not by the will & desire of a government."

" In the present instance it was pointed out to me that,
" independently of the wishes of Her Majesty's Government,
" there is legal authority to justify me in complying with
" the application. Three cases have been produced from
" the Records of this Court."

" The Third Case mentioned, which occurred in 1839,
" appears to furnish a more direct bearing. The Case was
" this :—Sir Herbert Taylor made a Codicil at Rome to his
" Will, the papers were proved here, & that Codicil was
" afterwards delivered out for the purpose of being sent to
" France, there to be placed in proper custody."

" On consideration, I think, I may be justified in follow-
" ing Sir Herbert Taylor's case, and granting the present
" application, but I cannot do so exactly in accordance with
" the precise form of the prayer, as I have not, I conceive,
" the power. I shall order the papers asked for to be
" delivered out, not for the purpose of their being sent to
" the French Government, but for the purpose of placing
" them in the Custody of the legal authorities in France,

"to be recorded in the proper place ; and I have no doubt
"that Lord John Russell will take care that this condition is
"complied with. I will direct the Registrar, after notarial
"copies have been made, to attend on his Lordship, and
"deliver the original papers to him, for which he must
"give a receipt. I think I am justified in going thus far,
"as in some respects, this Case is stronger than Sir Herbert
"Taylors. Sir Herbert was beyond doubt a domiciled
"Englishman, but Napoleon Bonaparte, though a prisoner
"at S⁺. Helena, did not, I conceive, from that circumstance
"lose his French domicile, moreover, his property in this
"Country was very small. Under all the circumstances of
"the case, I decree the original papers to be delivered out,
"in order that they may be sent, as in Taylor's case, to the
"legal Authorities in France."

The Queens Advocate intimated he could not pledge
himself, inasmuch as he had no authority to accept the
grant in any other form than that moved by him, that the
exact terms, specified by the Court, would be observed by
the Secretary of State. The Court stated it must adhere
to its decree, & could not presume that it would be dis-
regarded.

The application in the present case differs from the one
the Court has just referred to in the following particulars.

In that Case the Estate of The Emperor had long been
distributed & the Testamentary Papers in question were
no longer of pecuniary interest to anyone and the surviving executors of this will were consenting parties to the
application.

In the present case the entries in the Register may
involve the pecuniary interest of descendants of Families
named in it in tracing and establishing their rights to succession to property and it is therefore the duty of the
Court in making any order for its removal to other custody
to take especial care that such persons shall not be thereby
prejudiced. It is also a matter for observation that at the
time when the Manuscript was transmitted to Fulham
Palace the Bishop of London's Registry in Doctor's Common's was a legitimate place for depositing Registers or
Certificates of Marriages, Baptisms, & Deaths of persons
resident in the Colonies as well as of persons resident in
the London Diocese in England and that as on the Declara-

tion of Independence the Diocesan Registry ceased to be the Registry for Marriages, Baptisms, & Deaths in New England, in analogy to the practice in this Country when a New Diocese is carved out of an Old One a transfer of all documents in the Registry of the Old Diocese relating to the New Diocese is ordered to be made to the Registry of the New Diocese—the transmission of this Register to the Country to which it relates may be properly made. The Court will make a Decree for the transmission of this Manuscript Book to the Governor of the Commonwealth of Massachusetts in The United States of America subject to certain terms and conditions which I will settle in Chambers. Had this Manuscript been solely of Historical Value the Court would have had no hesitation in acting upon the precedent of The Library Company of Philadelphia referred to by M[r]. Statham who so liberally restored to this Country certain correspondence of National Interest which was deposited in that Library.

In the Consistory Court of London.

IN THE MATTER OF THE LOG OF THE MAYFLOWER.

SECOND JUDGMENT DELIVERED ON THE HANDING OVER OF "THE LOG" TO MR. BAYARD AT LONDON HOUSE ON THURSDAY, MAY 29TH, 1897.

In the Consistory Court of London.

IN THE MATTER OF THE LOG OF THE MAYFLOWER.

On Saturday the 10th of April an Application was made to me in the presence of the Lord Bishop of London and of the Registrar of the Court by M[r]. Henry White, Secretary to the American Embassy, on the instructions of the Hon[ble]. Colonel Hay, the present American Ambassador, for the Manuscript to be delivered over to Colonel Hay on his arrival in England, or to himself in the meantime, instead of to M[r]. Bayard, on the ground that M[r]. Bayard on his return from the Continent to England, when the delivery was to be made to him, would have ceased to be Ambassador here.

He stated, that if his Application was granted, the Manuscript would be transmitted with other State Papers to the President of the United States with a view to its transmission by the President to the Governor of Massachusetts to be deposited by him either in the State Archives or with the Historical Society in the City of Boston, in compliance with the Order of the Court. It appeared to me, that the application was a reasonable one, but I pointed out to M^r. White, that preliminary to my granting it, if it were in my power to do so, it would be necessary for a formal application to be made to me in open Court to vary the Decree in the manner suggested, & that if I acceded to this, it would be competent to any person alleging an interest in the matter, to appeal from the Amended Decree to the Arches and from thence to the Judicial Committee. Whereas the time for appealing from the original decree if it remained unaltered viz. 15 days from the date of its being made had expired. M^r. White thereupon said he would leave his application to be dealt with by me as I might deem right. I considered however, that the application having been made on the instructions of an Ambassador at the Court of S^t. James's it was only due to His Excellency, that I should maturely consider the question, & state on the present occasion whether it was or was not within powers discretionary or otherwise vested in the Court competent to it to make such a variation in the Decree. I have now come to the conclusion, that it would not be in accordance with the practice of the Court, or just to the parties interested in the Manuscript that I should so vary the original Decree.

In my Judgment I stated, that as the entries in the Register at the end of the Manuscript might involve the pecuniary interests of families named in it in tracing & establishing their rights to succession to property, it was the duty of the Court in making any Order for its removal to other Custody, to take especial care that such persons should not be thereby prejudiced. For my assistance in giving directions in the Registry as to the terms in which the Decree of the Court should be framed I obtained from the Principal Probate Registry a Copy of the Order made by the Prerogative Court of Canterbury for the delivery up of the Will & Codicils of The Emperor Napoleon I. as being the precedent on which I relied in granting the

Application in the present Case. The Order is dated February 17th, 1853, and is in the following terms " F. H. Dyke Her Majesty's Procurator General Exhibited Affidavit of the Rt Hon John Russell commonly called Lord John Russell and also Affidavit of John Allen Powell Esq and brought in Proxy of consent with Act of Court sped thereon and also statement in writing : The Judge having read the sd Affidavits and Statement at Petition of Dyke and on Motion of Her Majesty's Advocate directed the Original Will & Codicils of the said deceased now remaining in the Registry of this Court to be delivered into the possession Her Majesty's Secretary of State for Foreign Affairs by one of the Deputy Registrars of this Court for the purpose of being recorded or filed in the proper Court or with the legal authorities in France or a Notarial Copy of the said Will & Codicils being left in the Registry of this Court and assigned Dyke to bring in a Certificate of the said original Will and Codicils being recorded or filed as aforesaid. It is of importance for the purpose of preserving to persons interested in the entries in the Register at the end of the Manuscript the same right as they would have had if the Manuscript had remained under the control of the Court that the Decree of the Court should be so framed as to entitle them to enforce compliance with its provisions in the Courts of the United States after its transfer to that Country. According to the law on this point as stated by Mr. Justice Story in his great work on the Conflict of Laws : and the American Cases cited by him, it seems that compliance with the provisions of the Decree which will be read would be enforced in the Courts of the United States.

" The reasonable doctrine seems to be says Mr. Justice Story in order to found a proper ground of recognition of any Foreign Judgment in another Country that the Court pronouncing judgment should have complete jurisdiction over the cause, over the thing, and over the party (sec. 586). In proceeding in rem against movable property, within the jurisdiction of the Court pronouncing the Judgment whatever the Court settles as to the right or title or as to its disposition by transfer or other Act will be held valid in every other Country, where the same question comes directly or indirectly in Judgment before any other Tribunal (Sec. 592). In the present case the Manuscript or movable property is within the Jurisdiction of the Court and subject to its decrees. M^r. Bayard is also within its jurisdiction and will now undertake not as Ambassador, but as an individual to act as the Delegate of the Court in this matter in the place of the Registrar who primarily would be the proper Official to convey the Manuscript to the Governor of the Commonwealth of Massachusetts. M^r. White's proposal was that the Court should order the Manuscript to be delivered to Colonel Hay as Ambassador to be forwarded by him with the State Papers to The President of the United States, in order that it might be transmitted by the President to the Governor of The Commonwealth for the purposes named in the Decree. The objection to so varying the Decree is that the Court has no power to make an Order on the Head of a Sovereign State to carry out any of the provisions in its Decrees, & that such an Order, if made, would not be enforceable against the President, as far as my researches have gone, in the Courts of The United States at the instance of an aggrieved party.

Under these circumstances my duty will be to adhere to the Original Decree as directed by me and which is substantially in the terms of the Prayer of the Petition & with the Order of the Prerogative Court of Canterbury made in the matter of The Will & Codicils of The Emperor Napoleon I.

In the Consistory Court of London.

"LOG OF THE MAYFLOWER."

UNDERTAKING BY HON. THOMAS FRANCIS BAYARD.

In the Consistory Court of London.

IN THE MATTER OF THE ORIGINAL MANUSCRIPT OF THE BOOK ENTITLED AND KNOWN AS "THE LOG OF THE MAYFLOWER."

I THE HONORABLE THOMAS FRANCIS BAYARD lately Ambassador Extraordinary and Plenipotentiary of the United States of America at the Court of Saint James's London Do HEREBY UNDERTAKE in compliance with the Order of

this Honorable Court dated the Twelfth day of April 1897
and made on my Petition filed in the said Honorable Court,
that I will with all due care and diligence on my arrival
from England in the United States of America safely convey
over the original Manuscript Book known as and entitled
"The Log of the Mayflower" which has been this twenty
ninth day of April 1897 delivered over to me by the Lord
Bishop of London, to the City of Boston in the United
States of America and on my arrival in the said City deliver
the same over in person to the Governor of the Commonwealth of Massachusetts at his official Office in the State
House in the said City of Boston AND I FURTHER HEREBY
undertake from the time of the said delivery of the said
Book to me by the said Lord Bishop of London until I
shall have delivered the same to the Governor of Massachusetts to retain the same in my own personal custody.

T. F. BAYARD.

29th April 1897.

Over here there has been a little difficulty of understanding the principle on which the Consistory Court proceed.
If the surrender of the manuscript be ordered on the
ground that the property is not in the Bishop but that it
belongs to some person here, it would seem that the Court
could not impose conditions upon the surrender, or order
the manuscript delivered to the Governor or deposited in
the public archives of Massachusetts. On the other hand,
if there be no title established in any person other than the
Bishop, and he hold it in an official and not a personal
capacity as a public record, it is hard to see by what
authority any court, or even the Bishop himself, has power
to make the disposition found in the decree.

It is not important to settle this question. We certainly
have no disposition to look a gift horse in the mouth.
Still less have we the least desire to raise doubts of the
legality of what has occasioned such intense delight to all
of us. But we have no doubt his Lordship and the Court
well knew what they were about.

Perhaps the whole matter may be explained by considering the special power and function of the Judge of the Consistory Court. He is the Bishop's Vicar-General. His powers are not set forth, all of them, very fully in any text-book that we have been able to find. But they are of great antiquity and were well established in the usages of the Catholic Church long before the Reformation. The relation of the Vicar-General to the Bishop is much like that of the Chancellor to the Crown. In some cases his duties are purely judicial, binding the Bishop as the judicial action of the Chancellor binds the King and absolutely independent of any authority on the part of the Bishop to interfere with them as the judicial functions of the Chancellor are independent of any interference from the Crown. In all matters pertaining to the administration of justice, the authority of the Chancellor is as independent of that of the Crown as is the authority of the Court of King's Bench. There are other things, however, which the King does by his Chancellor. These are exertions of the royal authority, of the royal discretion, and sometimes of the royal benevolence. This distinction is well explained by the Supreme Court of the United States in the case of Fontain *v.* Ravenel, 17 How. p. 382.

The following statements of the powers and functions of Vicars-General may be found in a book now of high authority in the Catholic Church, viz. :

Elements of Ecclesiastical Law. Compiled with reference to the Syllabus, the "Const. Apostolicae Sedis" of Pope Pius IX., the Council of the Vatican and the latest Decisions of the Roman Congregations adapted especially to the Discipline of the Church in the United States. By Rev. S. B. Smith, D.D., formerly Professor of Canon Law, Author of "Notes," etc.

POWERS AND FUNCTIONS OF VICARS-GENERAL.

DEFINITION. A Vicar-General is one legitimately appointed to exercise, in a general way, episcopal jurisdiction in the Bishop's stead, in such manner that his acts are considered the acts of the Bishop himself. Smith, El. Eccles. Law, p. 340.

The Vicar-General's jurisdiction is, like the Bishop's, co-extensive with the diocese; it extends to all persons and matters within the diocese, and his acts have the same effect in law as if done by the Bishop himself. Id. p. 341.

JURISDICTION. As a general rule, the Vicar-General's jurisdiction extends to things temporal as well as to things spiritual. Although ordinarily appointed by the Bishop, he receives his jurisdiction from the common law. His powers, morally at least, are determined *certo et fixo modo, quem episcopus mutare nequit.* His appointment, *ipso facto,* confers upon him those powers, of which the scope cannot be altered or the exercise restrained by the Bishop, unless by removal.

APPEAL. Inasmuch as the V. G. represents in ecclesiastical law the person of the Bishop, it follows as a natural consequence that no appeal lies from a sentence of the V. G. to the Bishop *(a sententia vicarii generalis non datur ad episcopum appellatio).* But a petition may always be addressed to him for the remission of the penalty imposed by the V. G.   p. 343.

THE TRIBUNAL *(consistorium, auditoriam)* OF THE V. G. IS CONSIDERED IN ECCLESIASTICAL LAW THE TRIBUNAL OF THE BISHOP; THE PERSON OF THE V. G. THE PERSON OF THE BISHOP; AND THE SENTENCE PRONOUNCED BY THE V. G. THE SENTENCE OF THE BISHOP. Ib.

We understand that when the Bishop acts through his Vicar-General, in such cases the assent of the Bishop ordinarily must be obtained to the filing of the petition. After the jurisdiction is so gained, however, he is not permitted to interfere further with the decree; but he may be heard as a party in opposition, or may give his consent to the decree as any other party concerned.

REVEREND AND RIGHT HONORABLE
MANDELL CREIGHTON, D.D.,
Bishop of London.

It seems not unlikely, therefore, that the Consistory
Court treated this application as an application to transfer
the custody of a record of interest to the public to a place
of deposit where it would be more convenient of access to
the persons principally interested. It is as if it had been
found that some record or document in the possession of
the Bishop of London related wholly to titles or pedigrees
in Wales or Scotland, and an application had been made
to transfer the custody to the locality for such reason
deemed to be the most convenient. This would seem to
be a fair exercise of official discretion, supposing always
that no act of Parliament compelled the Bishop to retain
the custody. This explains the stress which is laid by the
court in its decree upon the fact found by him, that these
records may involve the pecuniary interest of descendants
of families named in it, in tracing and establishing their
rights to succession to property, etc. This seems to be
the foundation of the action of the court and explains the
conditions imposed in the decree.

DECREE OF THE CONSISTORIAL AND EPISCOPAL COURT OF
LONDON.

 MANDELL by Divine Permission LORD
BISHOP OF LONDON — To The Honor-
able THOMAS FRANCIS BAYARD Ambassador
Extraordinary and Plenipotentiary to Her
Most Gracious Majesty Queen Victoria at
the Court of Saint James's in London and
To The Governor and Commonwealth of Massachusetts in
the United States of America Greeting — WHEREAS a
Petition has been filed in the Registry of Our Consistorial
and Episcopal Court of London by you the said Honorable
Thomas Francis Bayard as Ambassador Extraordinary and
Plenipotentiary to Her Most Gracious Majesty Queen
Victoria at the Court of Saint James's in London on behalf
of the President and Citizens of the United States of
America wherein you have alleged that there is in Our
Custody as Lord Bishop of London a certain Manuscript

Book known as and entitled "The Log of the Mayflower"
containing an account as narrated by Captain William Bradford who was one of the Company of Englishmen who left
England in April 1620 in the ship known as "The Mayflower" of the circumstances leading to the prior Settlement
of that Company at Leyden in Holland their return to
England and subsequent departure for New England their
landing at Cape Cod in December 1620 their Settlement at
New Plymouth and their later history for several years
they being the Company whose Settlement in America is
regarded as the first real Colonisation of the New England
States and wherein you have also alleged that the said
Manuscript Book had been for many years past and was
then deposited in the Library attached to Our Episcopal
Palace at Fulham in the County of Middlesex and is of the
greatest interest importance and value to the Citizens of the
United States of America inasmuch as it is one of the earliest records of their national History and contains much
valuable information in regard to the original Settlers in
the States their family history and antecedents and that
therefore you earnestly desired to acquire possession of
the same for and on behalf of the President and Citizens of
the said United States of America AND WHEREIN you
have also alleged that you are informed that We as Lord
Bishop of London had fully recognised the value and interest of the said Manuscript Book to the Citizens of the
United States of America and the claims which they have
to its possession and that We were desirous of transferring
it to the said President and Citizens AND WHEREIN
you have also alleged that you are advised and believe that
the Custody of documents in the nature of public or ecclesiastical records belonging to the See of London is vested
in the Consistorial Court of the said See and that any disposal thereof must be authorised by an Order issued by
the Judge of that Honorable Court And that you therefore
humbly prayed that the said Honorable Court would deliver
to you the said Manuscript Book on your undertaking to
use every means in your power for the safe transmission
of the said Book to the United States of America and its
secure deposit and custody in the Pilgrim Hall at New
Plymouth or in such other place as may be selected by the
President and the Senate of the said United States and

upon such conditions as to security and access by and on
behalf of the English Nation as that Honorable Court
might determine AND WHEREAS the said Petition was
set down for hearing on one of the Court days in Hilary
Term to wit Thursday the Twenty fifth day of March One
thousand eight hundred and ninety seven in Our Consistorial Court in the Cathedral Church of Saint Paul in
London before The Right Worshipful Thomas Hutchinson
Tristram Doctor of Laws and one of Her Majesty's Counsel
learned in the Law Our Vicar General and Official Principal
the Judge of the said Court and you at the sitting of the
said Court appeared by Counsel in support of the Prayer
of the said Petition and during the hearing thereof the said
Manuscript Book was produced in the said Court by Our
legal Secretary and was then inspected and examined by the
said Judge and evidence was also given before the Court by
which it appeared that the Registry at Fulham Palace was
a Public Registry for Historical and Ecclesiastical Documents relating to the Diocese of London and to the Colonial and other possessions of Great Britain beyond the
Seas so long as the same remained by custom within the
said Diocese AND WHEREAS it appeared on the face of
the said Manuscript Book that the whole of the body
thereof with the exception of part of the last page thereof
was in the handwriting of the said William Bradford who
was elected Governor of New Plymouth in April 1621 and
continued Governor thereof from that date excepting
between the years 1635 and 1637 up to 1650 and that the
last five pages of the said Manuscript which is in the handwriting of the said William Bradford contain what in Law
is an authentic Register between 1620 and 1650 of the fact
of the Marriages of the Founders of the Colony of New
England with the names of their respective wives and
the names of their Children the lawful issue of such Marriages and of the fact of the Marriages of many of their
Children and Grandchildren and of the names of the issue
of such marriages and of the deaths of many of the persons named therein   And after hearing Counsel in support
of the said application the Judge being of opinion that the
said Manuscript Book had been upon the evidence before
the Court presumably deposited at Fulham Palace sometime
between the year 1729 and the year 1785 during which

time the said Colony was by custom within the Diocese of
London for purposes Ecclesiastical and the Registry of the
said Consistorial Court was a legitimate Registry for the
Custody of Registers of Marriages Births and Deaths within
the said Colony and that the Registry at Fulham Palace
was a registry for Historical and other Documents connected with the Colonies and possessions of Great Britain
beyond the Seas so long as the same remained by custom
within the Diocese of London and that on the Declaration of
the Independence of the United States of America in 1776
the said Colony had ceased to be within the Diocese of London and the Registry of the Court had ceased to be a public
registry for the said Colony and having maturely deliberated
on the Cases precedents and practice of the Ecclesiastical
Court bearing on the application before him and having
regard to the Special Circumstances of the Case Decreed
as follows — (1) That a Photographic facsimile reproduction of the said Manuscript Book verified by affidavit
as being a true and correct Photographic reproduction of
the said Manuscript Book be deposited in the Registry of
Our said Court by or on behalf of the Petitioner before
the delivery to the Petitioner of the said original Manuscript Book as hereinafter ordered — (2) That the said
Manuscript Book be delivered over to the said Honorable
Thomas Francis Bayard by the Lord Bishop of London or
in his Lordship's absence by the Registrar of the said
Court on his giving his undertaking in writing that he will
with all due care and diligence on his arrival from England
in the United States convey and deliver in person the said
Manuscript Book to the Governor of the Commonwealth
of Massachusetts in the United States of America at his
Official Office in the State House in the City of Boston and
that from the time of the delivery of the said Book to him
by the said Lord Bishop of London or by the said Registrar until he shall have delivered the same to the Governor
of Massachusetts he will retain the same in his own
Personal custody — (3) That the said Book be deposited
by the Petitioner with the Governor of Massachusetts for
the purpose of the same being with all convenient speed
finally deposited either in the State Archives of the
Commonwealth of Massachusetts in the City of Boston or
in the Library of the Historical Society of the said Com-

monwealth in the City of Boston as the Governor shall determine — (4) That the Governors of the said Commonwealth for all time to come be officially responsible for the safe custody of the said Manuscript Book whether the same be deposited in the State Archives at Boston or in the Historical Library in Boston aforesaid as well as for the performance of the following conditions subject to a compliance wherewith the said Manuscript Book is hereby decreed to be deposited in the Custody of the aforesaid Governor of the Commonwealth of Massachusetts and his Successors to wit : — (a) That all persons have such access to the said Manuscript Book as to the Governor of the said Commonwealth for the time being shall appear to be reasonable and with such safeguard as he shall order — (b) That all persons desirous of searching the said Manuscript Book for the bonâ fide purpose of establishing or tracing a Pedigree through persons named in the last five pages thereof or in any other part thereof shall be permitted to search the same under such safeguards as the Governor for the time being shall determine on payment of a fee to be fixed by the Governor — (c) That any person applying to the Official having the immediate custody of the said Manuscript Book for a Certified Copy of any entry contained in proof Marriage Birth or Death of persons named therein or of any other matter of like purport for the purpose of tracing descents shall be furnished with such certificate on the payment of a sum not exceeding one Dollar — (d) That with all convenient speed after the delivery of the said Manuscript Book to the Governor of the Commonwealth of Massachusetts the Governor shall transmit to the Registrar of the Court a Certificate of the delivery of the same to him by the Petitioner and that he accepts the Custody of the same subject to the terms and conditions herein named AND the Judge lastly decreed that the Petitioner on delivering the said Manuscript Book to the Governor aforesaid shall at the same time deliver to him this Our Decree Sealed with the Seal of the Court WHEREFORE WE the Bishop of London aforesaid well weighing and considering the premises DO by virtue of Our Authority Ordinary and Episcopal and as far as in Us lies and by Law We may or can ratify and confirm such Decree of Our Vicar General and

Official Principal of Our Consistorial and Episcopal Court of London IN TESTIMONY whereof We have caused the Seal of Our said Vicar General and Official Principal of the Consistorial and Episcopal Court of London which We use in this behalf to be affixed to these Presents DATED AT LONDON this Twelfth day of April One thousand eight hundred and ninety seven and in the first year of Our Translation.

HARRY W. LEE,

Exd. H.E.T. *Registrar.*

(L. S.)

RECEIPT OF HIS EXCELLENCY ROGER WOLCOTT.

RECEIPT OF GOVERNOR WOLCOTT.

His Excellency ROGER WOLCOTT, *Governor of the Commonwealth of Massachusetts, in the United States of America.*

To the Registrar of the Consistorial and Episcopal Court of London.

Whereas, The said Honorable Court, by its decree dated the twelfth day of April, 1897, and made on the petition of the Honorable Thomas Francis Bayard, lately Ambassador Extraordinary and Plenipotentiary of the United States of America at the Court of Saint James in London, did order that a certain original manuscript book then in the custody of the Lord Bishop of London, known as and entitled "The Log of the Mayflower," and more specifically described in said decree, should be delivered over to the said Honorable Thomas Francis Bayard by the Lord Bishop of London, on certain conditions specified in said decree, to be delivered by the said Honorable Thomas Francis Bayard in person to the Governor of the Commonwealth of Massachusetts, thereafter to be kept in the custody of the aforesaid Governor of the Commonwealth of Massachusetts and his successors, subject to a compliance with certain conditions, as set forth in said decree;

And Whereas, The said Honorable Court by its decree aforesaid did further order that, with all convenient speed after the delivery of the said manuscript book to the Governor of the Commonwealth of Massachusetts, the Governor should transmit to the Registrar of the said Honorable Court a certificate of the delivery of the same to him by the said Honorable Thomas Francis Bayard, and his acceptance of the custody of the same, subject to the terms and conditions named in the decree aforesaid;

Now, Therefore, In compliance with the decree aforesaid I do hereby certify that on the twenty-sixth day of May, 1897, the said Honorable Thomas Francis Bayard delivered in person to me, at my official office in the State House in the city of Boston, in the Commonwealth of Massachusetts, in the United States of America, a certain manuscript book which the said Honorable Thomas Francis Bayard then and there declared to be the original manuscript book known as and entitled "The Log of the Mayflower," which is more specifically described in the decree aforesaid: and I do further certify that I hereby accept the custody of the same, subject to the terms and conditions named in the decree aforesaid.

In witness whereof, I have hereunto signed my name and caused the seal of the Commonwealth to be affixed, at the Capitol in Boston, this twelfth day of July in the year of our Lord one thousand eight hundred and ninety-seven.

ROGER WOLCOTT.

By His Excellency the Governor,

WM. M. OLIN,
Secretary of the Commonwealth.

The following proceedings were had in the Representatives' Chamber at the State House in Boston, May 26, 1897, in the presence of the Governor, the Lieutenant Governor, the Executive Council, a Joint Convention of the two Houses of the Legislature and a large and brilliant concourse of citizens. Hon. George P. Lawrence, President of the Senate, presided.

ADDRESS OF SENATOR HOAR.

The first American ambassador to Great Britain, at the end of his official service, comes to Massachusetts on an interesting errand. He comes to deliver to the lineal successor of Governor Bradford, in the presence of the representatives and rulers of the body politic formed by the compact on board the "Mayflower," November 11, 1620, the only authentic history of the founding of their Commonwealth; the only authentic history of what we have a right to consider the most important political transaction that has ever taken place on the face of the earth.

Mr. Bayard has sought to represent to the mother country, not so much the diplomacy as the good-will of the American people. If in this anybody be tempted to judge him severely, let us remember what his great predecessor, John Adams, the first minister at the same court, representing more than any other man, embodying more than any other man, the spirit of Massachusetts, said to George III., on the first day of June, 1785, after the close of our long and bitter struggle for independence: "I shall esteem myself the happiest of men if I can be instrumental in restoring an entire esteem, confidence and affection, or, in better words, the old good-nature and the old good-humor between people who, though separated by an ocean and under different governments, have the same language, a similar religion and kindred blood."

And let us remember, too, the answer of the old monarch, who, with all his faults, must have had something of a noble and royal nature stirring in his bosom, when he replied: "Let the circumstances of language, religion and blood have their natural and full effect."

It has long been well known that Governor Bradford wrote and left behind him a history of the settlement of Plymouth. It was quoted by early chroniclers. There are extracts from it in the records at Plymouth. Thomas Prince used it when he compiled his "Annals." Hubbard depended on it when he wrote his "History of New England." Cotton Mather had read it, or a copy of a portion of it, when he wrote his "Magnalia." Governor Hutchinson had it when he published the second volume of his history in 1767. From that time it disappeared from the knowledge of everybody on this side of the water. All our historians speak of it as lost, and can only guess what had been its fate. Some persons suspected that it was destroyed when Governor Hutchinson's house was sacked in 1765, others that it was carried off by some officer or soldier when Boston was evacuated by the British army in 1776.

In 1844 Samuel Wilberforce, Bishop of Oxford, afterward Bishop of Winchester, one of the brightest of men, published one of the dullest and stupidest of books. It is entitled "The History of the Protestant Episcopal Church in America." It contained extracts from manuscripts which he said he had discovered in the library of the Bishop of London at Fulham. The book attracted no attention here until, about twelve years later, in 1855, John Wingate Thornton, whom many of us remember as an accomplished antiquary and a delightful gentleman, happened to pick up a copy of it while he was lounging in Burnham's book-store. He read the Bishop's quotations, and carried the book to his office, where he left it for his friend, Mr. Barry, who was then writing his "History of Massachusetts," with passages marked, and with a note which is not preserved, but which, according to his memory, suggested that the passages must have come from Bradford's long-lost history. That is the claim for Mr. Thornton. On the other hand, it is claimed by Mr. Barry that there was nothing of that kind expressed in Mr. Thornton's note, but in reading the book when he got it an hour or so later, the thought struck him for the first

time that the clew had been found to the precious book
which had been lost so long. He at once repaired to
Charles Deane, then and ever since, down to his death, as
President Eliot felicitously styled him, "the master of
historical investigators in this country." Mr. Deane saw
the importance of the discovery. He communicated at
once with Joseph Hunter, an eminent English scholar.
Hunter was high authority on all matters connected with
the settlement of New England. He visited the palace at
Fulham, and established beyond question the identity of
the manuscript with Governor Bradford's history, an original letter of Governor Bradford having been sent over for
comparison of handwriting.

How the manuscript got to Fulham nobody knows.
Whether it was carried over by Governor Hutchinson in
1774; whether it was taken as spoil from the tower of the
Old South Church in 1775; whether, with other manuscripts, it was sent to Fulham at the time of the attempts
of the Episcopal churches in America, just before the revolution, to establish an episcopate here,—nobody knows.
It would seem that Hutchinson would have sent it to the
colonial office; that an officer would naturally have sent it
to the war office; and a private would have sent it to the
war office, unless he had carried it off as mere private
booty and plunder,—in which case it would have been
unlikely that it would have reached a public place of
custody. But we find it in the possession of the church
and of the church official having, until independence was
declared, special jurisdiction over Episcopal interests in
Massachusetts and Plymouth. This may seem to point to
a transfer for some ecclesiastical purpose.

The Bishop's Chancellor conjectures that it was sent to
Fulham because of the record annexed to it of the early
births, marriages and deaths, such records being in England always in ecclesiastical custody. But this is merely
conjecture.

I know of no incident like this in history, unless it be the discovery in a chest in the castle of Edinburgh, where they had been lost for one hundred and eleven years, of the ancient regalia of Scotland,— the crown of Bruce, the sceptre and sword of state. The lovers of Walter Scott, who was one of the commissioners who made the search, remember his intense emotion, as described by his daughter, when the lid was removed. Her feelings were worked up to such a pitch that she nearly fainted, and drew back from the circle.

As she was retiring she was startled by his voice exclaiming, in a tone of the deepest emotion, "something between anger and despair," as she expressed it : "By God, no!" One of the commissioners, not quite entering into the solemnity with which Scott regarded this business, had, it seems, made a sort of motion as if he meant to put the crown on the head of one of the young ladies near him, but the voice and the aspect of the poet were more than sufficient to make this worthy gentleman understand his error : and, respecting the enthusiasm with which he had not been taught to sympathize, he laid down the ancient diadem with an air of painful embarrassment. Scott whispered, "Pray forgive me," and turning round at the moment observed his daughter deadly pale and leaning by the door. He immediately drew her out of the room, and when the air had somewhat recovered her, walked with her across Mound to Castle Street. "He never spoke all the way home," she says, "but every now and then I felt his arm tremble, and from that time I fancied he began to treat me more like a woman than a child. I thought he liked me better, too, than he had ever done before."

There have been several attempts to procure the return of the manuscript to this country. Mr. Winthrop, in 1860, through the venerable John Sinclair, Archdeacon, urged the Bishop of London to give it up, and proposed that the Prince of Wales, then just coming to this country, should take it across the Atlantic and present it to the people of Massachusetts. The Attorney-General, Sir Fitzroy Kelley, approved the plan, and said it would be an exceptional act of grace, a most interesting action, and that he heartily wished the success of the application. But the Bishop refused. Again, in 1869, John Lothrop Motley, then minister to England, who had a great and deserved influence there, repeated the proposition, at the suggestion of that most accomplished scholar, Justin Winsor. But his appeal had the same fate. The Bishop gave no encouragement, and said, as had been said nine years before, that the property could not be alienated without an act of Parliament. Mr. Winsor planned to repeat the attempt on his visit to England in 1877. When he was at Fulham the Bishop was absent, and he was obliged to go home without seeing him in person.

In 1881, at the time of the death of President Garfield, Benjamin Scott, Chamberlain of London, proposed again in the newspapers that the restitution should be made. But nothing came of it.

December 21, 1895, I delivered an address at Plymouth, on the occasion of the two hundred and seventy-fifth anniversary of the landing of the Pilgrims upon the rock. In preparing for that duty, I read again, with renewed enthusiasm and delight, the noble and touching story, as told by Governor Bradford. I felt that this precious history of the Pilgrims ought to be in no other custody than that of their children. But the case seemed hopeless. I found myself compelled by a serious physical infirmity to take a vacation, and to get a rest from public cares and duties, which was impossible while I stayed at home. When I went abroad I determined to visit the locality, on the borders of Lincolnshire and Yorkshire, from which Bradford and Brewster and Robinson, the three leaders of the Pilgrims, came, and where their first church was formed, and the places in Amsterdam and Leyden where the emi-

grants spent thirteen years. But I longed especially to
see the manuscript of Bradford at Fulham, which then
seemed to me, as it now seems to me, the most precious
manuscript on earth, unless we could recover one of the
four gospels as it came in the beginning from the pen of
the Evangelist.

The desire to get it back grew and grew during the
voyage across the Atlantic. I did not know how such a
proposition would be received in England. A few days
after I landed I made a call upon John Morley. I asked
him whether he thought the thing could be done. He
inquired carefully into the story, took down from his shelf
the excellent though brief life of Bradford in Leslie
Stephen's "Biographical Dictionary," and told me he
thought the book ought to come back to us, and that he
should be glad to do anything in his power to help. It
was my fortune, a week or two after, to sit next to Mr.
Bayard at a dinner given to Mr. Collins by the American
consuls in Great Britain. I took occasion to tell him the
story, and he gave me the assurance, which he has since
so abundantly and successfully fulfilled, of his powerful
aid. I was compelled, by the health of one of the party
with whom I was travelling, to go to the continent almost
immediately, and was disappointed in the hope of an early
return to England. So the matter was delayed until
about a week before I sailed for home, when I went to
Fulham, in the hope at least of seeing the manuscript. I
had supposed that it was a quasi-public library, open to
general visitors. But I found the Bishop was absent. I
asked for the librarian, but there was no such officer, and
I was told very politely that the library was not open to
the public, and was treated in all respects as that of a
private gentleman. So I gave up any hope of doing anything in person. But I happened the Friday before I
sailed for home to dine with an English friend who had
been exceedingly kind to me. As he took leave of me,

7

about eleven o'clock in the evening, he asked me if there was anything more he could do for me. I said, "No, unless you happen to know the Lord Bishop of London. I should like to get a sight at the manuscript of Bradford's history before I go home." He said, "I do not know the Bishop myself, but Mr. Grenfell, at whose house you spent a few days in the early summer, is the Bishop's nephew by marriage, and will gladly give you an introduction to his uncle. He is in Scotland. But I will write to him before I go to bed."

Sunday morning brought me a cordial letter from Mr. Grenfell, introducing me to the Bishop. I wrote a note to his lordship, saying I should be glad to have an opportunity to see Bradford's history: that I was to sail for the United States the next Wednesday, but would be pleased to call at Fulham Tuesday, if that were agreeable to him.

I got a note in reply, in which he said if I would call on Tuesday he would be happy to show me "The Log of the Mayflower," which is the title the English, without the slightest reason in the world, give the manuscript. I kept the appointment, and found the Bishop with the book in his hand. He received me with great courtesy, showed me the palace, and said that that spot had been occupied by a Bishop's palace for more than a thousand years.

After looking at the volume and reading the records on the flyleaf, I said: "My lord, I am going to say something which you may think rather audacious. I think this book ought to go back to Massachusetts. Nobody knows how it got over here. Some people think it was carried off by Governor Hutchinson, the Tory governor: other people think it was carried off by British soldiers when Boston was evacuated; but in either case the property would not have changed. Or, if you treat it as a booty, in which last case, I suppose, by the law of nations ordinary property does change, no civilized nation in modern

FULHAM PALACE. S.W.

21 Sept. 1896

The Bishop of London presents his compliments to Senator Hoar and will be glad to show him the log of the Mayflower at 11. a.m tomorrow (Tuesday) if he will be good to call here for the purpose

times applies that principle to the property of libraries and institutions of learning."

"Well," said the Bishop, "I did not know you cared anything about it."

"Why," said I, "if there were in existence in England a history of King Alfred's reign for thirty years, written by his own hand, it would not be more precious in the eyes of Englishmen than this manuscript is to us."

"Well," said he, "I think myself it ought to go back, and if it depended on me it would have gone back before this. But the Americans who have been here — many of them have been commercial people — did not seem to care much about it except as a curiosity. I suppose I ought not to give it up on my own authority. It belongs to me in my official capacity, and not as private or personal property. I think I ought to consult the Archbishop of Canterbury. And, indeed," he added, "I think I ought to speak to the Queen about it. We should not do such a thing behind Her Majesty's back."

I said: "Very well. When I go home I will have a proper application made from some of our literary societies, and ask you to give it consideration."

I saw Mr. Bayard again, and told him the story. He was at the train when I left London for the steamer at Southampton. He entered with great interest into the matter, and told me again he would gladly do anything in his power to forward it.

When I got home I communicated with Secretary Olney about it, who took a kindly interest in the matter, and wrote to Mr. Bayard that the administration desired he should do everything in his power to promote the application. The matter was then brought to the attention of the Council of the American Antiquarian Society, the Massachusetts Historical Society, the Pilgrim Society of Plymouth and the New England Society of New York. These bodies appointed committees to unite in the application. Gov-

ernor Wolcott was also consulted, who gave his hearty
approbation to the movement, and a letter was dispatched
through Mr. Bayard.

Meantime Bishop Temple, with whom I had my conversation, had himself become Archbishop of Canterbury,
and in that capacity Primate of all England. His successor, Rev. Dr. Creighton, had been the delegate of John
Harvard's College to the great celebration at Harvard University in 1886, on the two hundred and fiftieth anniversary of its foundation. He had received the degree of
doctor of laws from the university, had been a guest of
President Eliot, and had received President Eliot as his
guest in England.

He is an accomplished historical scholar, and very
friendly in sentiment to the people of the United States.
So, by great good fortune, the two eminent ecclesiastical
personages who were to have a powerful influence in the
matter were likely to be exceedingly well disposed. Dr.
Benjamin A. Gould, the famous mathematician, was
appointed one of the committee of the American Antiquarian Society. He died suddenly, just after a letter to the
Bishop of London was prepared and about to be sent to
him for signing. He took a very zealous interest in the
matter. The letter formally asked for the return of the
manuscript, and was signed by the following-named gentlemen : George F. Hoar, Stephen Salisbury, Edward Everett
Hale, Samuel A. Green, for the American Antiquarian
Society ; Charles Francis Adams, William Lawrence,
Charles W. Eliot, for the Massachusetts Historical Society ;
Arthur Lord, William M. Evarts, William T. Davis, for
the Pilgrim Society of Plymouth ; Charles C. Beaman,
Joseph H. Choate, J. Pierpont Morgan, for the New
England Society of New York : Roger Wolcott, Governor
of Massachusetts.

The rarest good fortune seems to have attended every
step in this transaction.

THE RIGHT HONORABLE AND MOST REVEREND
FREDERICK TEMPLE, D.D.,
Archbishop of Canterbury.

I was fortunate in having formed the friendship of Mr. Grenfell, which secured to me so cordial a reception from the Bishop of London.

It was fortunate that the Bishop of London was Dr. Temple, an eminent scholar, kindly disposed toward the people of the United States, and a man thoroughly capable of understanding and respecting the deep and holy sentiment which a compliance with our desire was to gratify.

It was fortunate, too, that Bishop Temple, who thought he must have the approbation of the Archbishop before his action, when the time came had himself become Archbishop of Canterbury and Primate of all England.

It was fortunate that Dr. Creighton had succeeded to the see of London. He is, himself, as I have just said, an eminent historical scholar. He has many friends in America. He was the delegate of Emmanuel, John Harvard's College, at the great Harvard celebration in 1886. He received the degree of doctor of laws at Harvard and is a member of the Massachusetts Historical Society and the American Antiquarian Society. He had, as I have said, entertained President Eliot as his guest in England.

It was fortunate, too, that the application came in a time of cordial good-will between the two countries, when the desire of John Adams and the longing of George III. have their ample and complete fulfilment. This token of the good-will of England reached Boston on the eve of the birthday of the illustrious sovereign, who is not more venerated and beloved by her own subjects than by the kindred people across the sea.

It comes to us at the time of the rejoicing of the English people at the sixtieth anniversary of a reign more crowded with benefit to humanity than any other known in the annals of the race. Upon the power of England, the sceptre, the trident, the lion, the army and the fleet, the monster ships of war, the all-shattering guns, the American people are strong enough now to look with an entire indifference. We encounter her commerce and her manufactures in the spirit of a generous emulation. The inheritance from which England has learned these things is ours also. We, too, are of the Saxon strain.

> In our halls is hung
> Armoury of the invincible knights of old.

Our temple covers a continent, and its porches are upon both the seas. Our fathers knew the secret to lay, in Christian liberty and law, the foundations of empire. Our young men are not ashamed, if need be, to speak with the enemy in the gate.

But to the illustrious lady, type of gentlest womanhood, model of mother and wife and friend, who came at eighteen to the throne of George IV. and William; of purer eyes than to behold iniquity; the maiden presence before which everything unholy shrank; the sovereign who, during her long reign, "ever knew the people that she ruled"; the royal nature that disdained to strike at her kingdom's rival in the hour of our sorest need; the heart which even in the bosom of a queen beat with sympathy for the cause of constitutional liberty; who, herself not unacquainted with grief, laid on the coffin of our dead Garfield the wreath fragrant with a sister's sympathy, — to her our republican manhood does not disdain to bend.

> The eagle, lord of land and sea,
> Will stoop to pay her fealty.

But I am afraid this application might have had the fate of its predecessors but for our special good fortune in the fact that Mr. Bayard was our Ambassador at the Court of St. James. He had been, as I said in the beginning, the ambassador not so much of the diplomacy as of the goodwill of the American people. Before his powerful influence every obstacle gave way. It was almost impossible for Englishmen to refuse a request like this, made by him, and in which his own sympathies were so profoundly enlisted.

You are entitled, sir, to the gratitude of Massachusetts, to the gratitude of every lover of Massachusetts and of every lover of the country. You have succeeded where so many others have failed, and where so many others would have been likely to fail. You may be sure that our debt to you is fully understood and will not be forgotten.

The question of the permanent abiding-place of this manuscript will be settled after it has reached the hands of His Excellency. Wherever it shall go it will be an object of reverent care. I do not think many Americans will gaze upon it without a little trembling of the lips and a little gathering of mist in the eyes, as they think of the story of suffering, of sorrow, of peril, of exile, of death and of lofty triumph which that book tells, — which the hand of the great leader and founder of America has traced on those pages.

There is nothing like it in human annals since the story of Bethlehem. These Englishmen and Englishwomen going out from their homes in beautiful Lincoln and York, wife separating from husband and mother from child in that hurried embarkation for Holland, pursued to the beach by English horsemen; the thirteen years of exile; the life at Amsterdam "in alley foul and lane obscure"; the dwelling at Leyden; the embarkation at Delfthaven; the farewell of Robinson: the terrible voyage across the Atlantic; the compact in the harbor; the landing on the rock; the dreadful first winter; the death roll of more than half the number; the days of suffering and of famine; the wakeful night, listening for the yell of wild beast and the war-whoop of the savage; the building of the State on those sure foundations which no wave or tempest has ever shaken; the breaking of the new light; the dawning of the new day; the beginning of the new life; the enjoyment of peace with liberty,—of all these things this is the original record by the hand of our beloved father and founder. Massachusetts will preserve it until the time shall come that her children are unworthy of it; and that time shall come,—never.

ADDRESS OF AMBASSADOR BAYARD.

YOUR EXCELLENCY, GENTLEMEN OF THE TWO HOUSES OF THE LEGISLATURE OF MASSACHUSETTS, LADIES AND GENTLEMEN, FELLOW-COUNTRYMEN : The honorable and most gratifying duty with which I am charged is about to receive its final act of execution, for I have the book here, and here I produce it as it was placed in my hands by the Lord Bishop of London on April 29, intact then and now ; and I am about to deliver it according to the provisions of the decree of the Chancellor of London, which has been read in your presence, and the receipt signed by me and registered in his court that I would obey the provisions of that decree.

I have kept my trust ; I have kept the book as I received it ; I shall deliver it into the hands of the representative of the people who are entitled to its custody.

And now, gentlemen, it would be superfluous for me to dwell upon the historical features of this remarkable occasion, for it has been done, as we all knew it would be done, with ability, learning, eloquence and impressiveness, by the distinguished Senator who represents you so well in the Congress of the United States.

For all that related to myself, and for every gracious word of recognition and commendation that fell from his lips in relation to the part that I have taken in the act of restoration, I am profoundly grateful. It is an additional reward, but not the reward which induced my action.

To have served your State, to have been instrumental in such an act of this, was of itself a high privilege to me. The Bradford Manuscript was in the library of Fulham palace, and if, by lawful means, I could have become possessed of the volume, and could have brought it here and quietly deposited it, I should have gone to my home with the great satisfaction of knowing that I had performed an act of justice, an act of right between two countries. Therefore the praise, however grateful, is additional, and I am very thankful for it.

It may not be inappropriate or unpleasing to you should I state in a very simple manner the history of my relation to the return of this book, for it all has occurred within the last twelve months.

I knew of the existence of this manuscript; I had seen the reproduction in facsimile. I knew that attempts had been made unsuccessfully to obtain the original book.

At that time Senator Hoar made a short visit to England, and in passing through London I was informed by him of the great interest that he, in common with the people of this State, had in the restoration of this manuscript to the custody of the State.

We discussed the methods by which it might be accomplished, and after two or three mutually concurrent suggestions he returned to the United States, and presently I received, under cover from the Secretary of State, — a distinguished citizen of your own State, Mr. Olney, — a formal note, suggesting rather than instructing that in an informal manner I should endeavor to have carried out the wishes of the various societies who had addressed themselves to the Bishop of London and the Archbishop of Canterbury, in order to obtain the return of this manuscript.

It necessarily had to be done informally. The strict regulations of the office I then occupied forbade my correspondence with any member of the British government except through the foreign office, unless it were informal. An old saying describes the entire case, that "Where there's a will there's a way." There certainly was the will to get the book, and there certainly was also a will and a way to give the book, and that way was discovered by the legal custodians of the book itself.

At first there were suggestions of some difficulty, some technical questions ; and following a rule, and a very safe rule, the first thought was, What is the law? and the case was submitted to the law officers of the Crown. Then there became the necessity of an act of permission.

There was to be entertained no question as to the title to the manuscript in the possession of the British government. There was no authority to grant a claim, founded on adverse title, and the question arose for a form of law of a permissive rather than of a mandatory nature, in order for it to be authoritative with those who had charge of the document.

But, as I said, when there was a will there was found a way. By personal correspondence, by personal interviews with the Bishop of London, I soon discovered that he was as anxious to find the way as I was that he should find it. In the month of last March it was finally agreed that I should employ legal counsel to present formal petition and proceeding in the Episcopal Consistorial Court of London, and there before the Chancellor to lay the strong desire of Massachusetts and her people for the return of the record of her early Governor.

Accordingly, the petition was prepared, and by my authority signed as for me by an eminent member of the bar, and that petition was also signed by the Bishop of London, so that there was a complete consensus. The decree was ordered as it is published in the London "Times" on March 25 last, and nothing after that remained but formalities, in which, as you are well aware, the English law is not lacking, especially in the ecclesiastical tribunals.

These formalities were carried out during my absence from London on a short visit, and the decree which you have heard read was duly entered on April 12 last, consigning the document to my personal custody, to be delivered by me in this city to the high official therein

named, subject to those conditions which you have also
heard.

Accordingly, on the 29th of April I was summoned to
the court, and there, having signed the receipt, this decree
was read in my presence. There the Bishop of London
arose, and, taking the book in his hands, delivered it with
a few gracious words into my custody, and here it is to-day.

The records of those proceedings will no doubt be preserved here as accompanying this book, as they are of the
Episcopal Consistorial Court in London, and they tell the
entire story.

But that is but part. The thing that I wish to impress
upon you, and upon my fellow-countrymen throughout the
United States, is that this is an act of courtesy and friendship by another government — the government of what we
once called our "mother country" — to the entire people of
the United States.

You cannot limit it to the Governor of the Commonwealth ; you cannot limit it to the Legislature ; you cannot
limit it to the citizens of this Commonwealth. It extends
in its courtesy, in its kindness and comity to the entire
people of the United States. From first to last there was
the ready response of courtesy and kindness to the request
for the restoration of this manuscript record.

I may say to you that there has been nothing that I have
sought more earnestly than to place the affairs of these
two great nations in the atmosphere of mutual confidence
and respect and good-will. If it be a sin to long for the
honor of one's country, for the safety and strength of one's
country, then I have been a great sinner, for I have striven
to advance the honor and the safety and the welfare of my
country, and believed it was best accomplished by treating
all with justice and courtesy, and doing those things to
others which we would ask to have done to ourselves.

When the Chancellor pronounced his decree in March
last, he cited certain precedents to justify him in restoring

this volume to where it belongs. One precedent which powerfully controlled his decision, and which in the closing portion of his judgment he emphasizes, was an act of generous liberality upon the part of the Library Company of Philadelphia in voluntarily returning to the British government some volumes of original manuscript of the period of James the First which by some means not very clearly explained had found their way among the books of that institution.

Those books were received by a very distinguished man, Lord Romilly, Master of the Rolls, who took occasion to speak of the liberality and kindness which dictated the action of the Philadelphia library. Gentlemen, I am one of those who believe that a generous and kindly act is never unwise between individuals or nations.

The return of this book to you is an echo to the kindly act of your countrymen in the city of Philadelphia in 1866.

It is that; not, as Mr. Hoar has said, any influence or special effort of mine; but it is the desire to enlist international good feeling and comity which brought about to you the pleasure and the joy of having this manuscript returned, and so it will ever be. A generous act will beget a generous act; trust and confidence will beget trust and confidence; and so it will be while the world shall last, and well will it be for the man or for the people who shall recognize this truth and act upon it.

Now, gentlemen, there is another coincidence that I may venture to point out. It is history repeating itself. More than three hundred years ago the ancestors from whom my father drew his name and blood were French Protestants, who were compelled to flee from the religious persecutions of that day, and for the sake of conscience to find an asylum in Holland. Fifty years after they had fled and found safety in Holland, the little congregation of Independents from the English village of Scrooby, under the pastorate of John Robinson, were forced to fly, and with difficulty found their way into the same country of the Netherlands, seeking an asylum for their consciences' sake. Time passed on. The little English colony removed, as the history in this manuscript of William Bradford will tell you, across the Atlantic, and soon after the Huguenot family from whom I drew my name found their first settlement in what was then the New Netherlands, now New York. Both came from the same cause; both came with the same object, the same purpose,—"soul freedom," as Roger Williams well called it. Both came to found homes where they could worship God according to their own conscience and live as free men. They came to these shores, and they have found the asylum, and they have strengthened it, and it is what we see today,—a country of absolute religious and civil freedom,—of equal rights and toleration.

And is it not fitting that I, who have in my veins the blood of the Huguenots, should present to you and your Governor the log of the English emigrants, who left their country for the sake of religious freedom?   .

They are blended here,—their names, their interests. No man asks and no man has a right to ask or have ascertained by any method authorized by law what is the conscientious religious tenet or opinion of any man, of any citizen, as a prerequisite for holding an office of trust or power in the United States.

I think it well on this occasion to make, as I am sure you are making, acknowledgment to that heroic little country, the Lowlands as they call it, the Netherlands,—the country without one single feature of military defence except the brave hearts of the men who live in it and defend it.

Holland was the anvil upon which religious and civil liberty was beaten out in Europe at a time when the clang was scarcely heard anywhere else. We can never forget our historical debt to that country and to those people.

Puritan, Independent, Huguenot, whoever he may be, fleeing or forced to flee for conscience's sake, will not forget that in the Netherlands there was found in his time of need the asylum where conscience, property and person might be secure.

And now my task is done. I am deeply grateful for the part that I have been enabled to take in this act of just and natural restitution. In Massachusetts or out of Massachusetts there is no one more willing than I to assist this work; and here, sir [addressing Governor Wolcott], I fulfil my trust in presenting to you the manuscript.

To you, as the honored representative of the people of this Commonwealth, I commit this book, in pursuance of my obligations, gladly undertaken under the decree of the Episcopal Consistorial Court of London.

ADDRESS OF GOVERNOR WOLCOTT.

On receiving the volume, Governor Wolcott, addressing Mr. Bayard, spoke as follows: I thank you, sir, for the diligent and faithful manner in which you have executed the honorable trust imposed upon you by the decree of the Consistorial and Episcopal Court in London, a copy of which you have now placed in my hands. It was fitting that one of your high distinction should be selected to perform so dignified an office.

The gracious act of international courtesy which is now completed will not fail of grateful appreciation by the people of this Commonwealth and of the Nation. It is honorable alike to those who hesitated not to prefer the request and to those whose generous liberality has prompted compliance with it. It may be that the story of the departure of this precious work from our shores may never in its every detail be revealed; but the story of its return will be read of all men, and will become a part of the

history of the Commonwealth. There are places and
objects so intimately associated with the world's greatest
men or with mighty deeds that the soul of him who gazes
upon them is lost in a sense of reverent awe, as it listens
to the voice that speaks from the past, in words like those
which came from the burning bush, "Put off thy shoes
from off thy feet, for the place whereon thou standest is
holy ground."

On the sloping hillside of Plymouth, that bathes its feet
in the waters of the Atlantic, such a voice is breathed by
the brooding genius of the place, and the ear must be dull
that fails to catch the whispered words. For here not
alone did godly men and women suffer greatly for a great
cause, but their noble purpose was not doomed to defeat,
but was carried to perfect victory. They established what
they planned. Their feeble plantation became the birth-
place of religious liberty, the cradle of a free Commonwealth. To them a mighty nation owns its debt. Nay,
they have made the civilized world their debtor. In the
varied tapestry which pictures our national life, the richest
spots are those where gleam the golden threads of conscience, courage and faith, set in the web by that little
band. May God in his mercy grant that the moral impulse
which founded this nation may never cease to control its
destiny: that no act of any future generation may put in
peril the fundamental principles on which it is based, — of
equal rights in a free state, equal privileges in a free church
and equal opportunities in a free school.

In this precious volume which I hold in my hands — the
gift of England to the Commonwealth of Massachusetts —
is told the noble, simple story of the Plymouth Plantation.
In the midst of suffering and privation and anxiety the
pious hand of William Bradford here set down in ample
detail the history of the enterprise from its inception to the
year 1647. From him we may learn "that all great and
honourable actions are accompanied with great difficulties,

and must be both enterprised and overcome with answerable courages."

The sadness and pathos which some might read into the narrative are to me lost in victory. The triumph of a noble cause even at a great price is theme for rejoicing and not for sorrow. And the story here told is one of triumphant achievement, and not of defeat.

As the official representative of the Commonwealth, I receive it, sir, at your hands. I pledge the faith of the Commonwealth that for all time it shall be guarded in accordance with the terms of the decree under which it is delivered into her possession as one of her chiefest treasures. I express the thanks of the Commonwealth for the priceless gift. And I venture the prophecy that for countless years to come and to untold thousands these mute pages shall eloquently speak of high resolve, great suffering and heroic endurance made possible by an absolute faith in the over-ruling providence of Almighty God.

PROCEEDINGS OF THE LEGISLATURE.

JOURNAL OF THE SENATE.

Monday, May 24, 1897.

The following message from His Excellency the Governor came up from the House, to wit :—

Boston, *May 22, 1897.*

To the Honorable Senate and House of Representatives.

I have the honor to call to your attention the fact that Wednesday, May 26, at 11 A. M., has been fixed as the date of the formal presentation to the Governor of the Commonwealth of the Bradford Manuscript History, recently ordered by decree of the Consistory Court of the Diocese of London to be returned to the Commonwealth of Massachusetts by the hands of the Honorable Thomas F. Bayard, lately Ambassador at the Court of St. James; and to suggest for the favorable consideration of your honorable bodies that the exercises of presentation be held in the House of Representatives on the day and hour above given, in the presence of a joint convention of the two bodies and of invited guests and the public.

ROGER WOLCOTT.

Thereupon, on motion of Mr. Roe,—

Ordered, That, in accordance with the suggestion of His Excellency the Governor, a joint convention of the two branches be held in the chamber of the House of Representatives, on Wednesday, May the twenty-sixth, at eleven o'clock A. M., for the purpose of witnessing the exercises of the formal presentation, to the Governor of the Commonwealth, of the Bradford Manuscript History, recently ordered by decree of the Consistory Court of the Diocese of London to be returned to the Commonwealth of Massachusetts by the hands of the Honorable Thomas F. Bayard, lately Ambassador at the Court of St. James; and further

Ordered, That the clerks of the two branches give notice to His Excellency the Governor of the adoption of this order.

Sent down for concurrence. (It was concurred with on the same day.)

JOURNAL OF THE SENATE.

WEDNESDAY, MAY 26, 1897.

Joint Convention.

At eleven o'clock A. M., pursuant to assignment, the two branches met in

CONVENTION

in the Chamber of the House of Representatives.

On motion of Mr. Roe,—

Ordered, That a committee, to consist of three members of the Senate and eight members of the House of Representatives, be appointed, to wait upon His Excellency the

8

Governor and inform him that the two branches are now
in convention for the purpose of witnessing the exercises
of the formal presentation, to the Governor of the Commonwealth, of the Bradford Manuscript History.

Messrs. Roe, Woodward and Gallivan, of the Senate,
and Messrs. Pierce of Milton, Bailey of Plymouth, Brown
of Gloucester, Fairbank of Warren, Bailey of Newbury,
Sanderson of Lynn, Whittlesey of Pittsfield and Bartlett
of Boston, of the House, were the committee.

Mr. Roe, from the committee, afterwards reported that
they had attended to the duty assigned them, and that His
Excellency the Governor had been pleased to say that he
received the message and should be pleased to wait upon
the Convention forthwith for the purpose named.

His Excellency the Governor, accompanied by His
Honor the Lieutenant-Governor and the Honorable Coun-
cil, and by the Honorable Thomas F. Bayard, lately
Ambassador of the United States at the Court of St.
James's, the Honorable George F. Hoar, Senator from
Massachusetts in the Congress of the United States, and
other invited guests, entered the chamber.

The decree of the Consistorial and Episcopal Court of
London, authorizing the return of the manuscript and its
delivery to the Governor, was read.

The President then presented the Honorable George F.
Hoar, who gave an account of the manuscript and of the
many efforts that had been made to secure its return.

The Honorable Thomas F. Bayard was then introduced
by the President, and he formally presented the manuscript
to His Excellency the Governor, who accepted it in behalf
of the Commonwealth.

On motion of Mr. Bradford, the following order was
adopted :—

Whereas, In the presence of the Senate and of the House
of Representatives in joint convention assembled, and in
accordance with a decree of the Consistorial and Episcopal
Court of London, the manuscript of Bradford's "History
of the Plimouth Plantation" has this day been delivered to

His Excellency the Governor of the Commonwealth by the Honorable Thomas F. Bayard, lately Ambassador of the United States at the Court of St. James; and

Whereas, His Excellency the Governor has accepted the said manuscript in behalf of the Commonwealth; therefore, be it

Ordered, That the Senate and the House of Representatives of the Commonwealth of Massachusetts place on record their high appreciation of the generous and gracious courtesy that prompted this act of international good-will, and express their grateful thanks to all concerned therein, and especially to the Lord Bishop of London, for the return to the Commonwealth of this precious relic; and be it further

Ordered, That His Excellency the Governor be requested to transmit an engrossed and duly authenticated copy of this order with its preamble to the Lord Bishop of London.

His Excellency, accompanied by the other dignitaries, then withdrew, the Convention was dissolved, and the Senate returned to its chamber.

Subsequently a resolve was passed (approved June 10, 1897) providing for the publication of the history from the original manuscript, together with a report of the proceedings of the joint convention, such report to be prepared by a committee consisting of one member of the Senate and two members of the House of Representatives, and to include, so far as practicable, portraits of His Excellency Governor Roger Wolcott, William Bradford, the Honorable George F. Hoar, the Honorable Thomas F. Bayard, the Archbishop of Canterbury and the Lord Bishop of London; facsimiles of the pages from the manuscript history, and a picture of the book itself; copies of the decree of the Consistorial and Episcopal Court of London, the receipt of the Honorable Thomas F. Bayard for the manuscript, and the receipt sent by His Excellency the Governor to the Consistorial and Episcopal Court; an account of the legislative action taken with reference to the presentation and reception of the manuscript; the addresses

of the Honorable George F. Hoar, the Honorable Thomas
F. Bayard and His Excellency Governor Roger Wolcott;
and such other papers and illustrations as the committee
might deem advisable; the whole to be printed under the
direction of the Secretary of the Commonwealth, and the
book distributed by him according to directions contained
in the resolve.

Senator Alfred S. Roe of Worcester and Representatives
Francis C. Lowell of Boston and Walter L. Bouvé of
Hingham were appointed as the committee.